Loyalty Is Everything 3

Molotti

**Lock Down Publications and Ca$h
Presents**

Loyalty Is Everything 3

A Novel by *Molotti*

Molotti

Lock Down Publications
Po Box 944
Stockbridge, Ga 30281

Visit our website @
www.lockdownpublications.com

Lock Down Publications
Like our page on Facebook: Lock Down Publications @
www.facebook.com/lockdownpublications.ldp
Book interior design by: **Shawn Walker**
Edited by: **Kiera Northington**

Stay Connected with Us!

Text **LOCKDOWN** to 22828 to stay up-to-date with new releases, sneak peaks, contests and more…
Thank you.

Submission Guideline.

Submit the first three chapters of your completed manuscript to ldpsubmissions@gmail.com, subject line: Your book's title. The manuscript must be in a .doc file and sent as an attachment. Document should be in Times New Roman, double spaced and in size 12 font. Also, provide your synopsis and full contact information. If sending multiple submissions, they must each be in a separate email.

Have a story but no way to send it electronically? You can still submit to LDP/Ca$h Presents. Send in the first three chapters, written or typed, of your completed manuscript to:

LDP: Submissions Dept
Po Box 944
Stockbridge, Ga 30281

DO NOT send original manuscript. Must be a duplicate.

Provide your synopsis and a cover letter containing your full contact information.

Thanks for considering LDP and Ca$h Presents.

DEDICATIONS

This one is dedicated to Paradise,Tahj, Zion, Dj and Taylen. And to Big Red, I know for a fact that you would've been proud of me. Rest up Queen I Love you and I miss you.

ACKNOWLEDGMENTS

Once again all thanks and praises go to the man up top. Grateful would be an understatement of what I am. I would also like to thank the person who taught me that 'Loyalty Is Everything. You know who you are. Who would've thought that those three words would turn into all this? I was able to take those three words and turn them into Success so thank you. Special thanks to my brother Von D for pushing my shit like nobody else, I love you lil bro. Thanks to everyone who's been supporting me, I'm grateful for all the love y'all been showing. Thanks to all the men in the Illinois state prisons, Cook County jail and the Feds that read any of my books and pushed me to keep writing and put this shit out there, y'all were the first ones who believed in me My boy Banks (Madville), Teflon (Moe Town), Zo (Lafa), Big Deon (Calumet buildings), TVL Rondo (Chicago Ave and Waller) J-Nate (P-Town), C1 (Northpole), Tido (Moe Town), Fox (Lo Block), Gambling Ass Chucky, Lil Dave (Sane Gang) and everybody else who was fucking with me, without y'all I wouldn't have made it this far so thanks. FREE THE REAL!

Molotti

Chapter 1

The moonlight gleamed off the diamonds on Blake's bust down Cartier wristwatch as he lifted his bottle of Dussé to his lips and took a healthy swig. The liquor burned going down his throat, but he embraced the burn, he welcomed it. He was sitting at the cemetery talking to Lil Ced's headstone. He had been at the cemetery for well over an hour, he spent some time at his brother Six's grave and then decided to come holla at Lil Ced before he left. The cemetery was where he went to find peace of mind.

Whenever life got too hectic, or he needed to clear his mind the cemetery was where he ran to. He felt alone everywhere else but not here. His little brother and his best friend were the two people who understood him the most, so whenever his plate got too full, he ran to them with his problems. Now was one of those times where Blake had absolutely too much going on in his life. He was at war with the Latin Kings, as well as a handful of different hoods throughout the city. He was also into it with his right-hand man, KD, over a bitch who he really shouldn't have been fucking in the first place.

Not only that, but Blake had really begun to catch feelings for Aisha, even though he was in a whole relationship. And on top of all that, he was the interim head of Aisha's father, Cordale's drug operation, which was doing way better when Blake was just a worker instead of the boss. As of late, nothing seemed to be going Blake's way.

Blake took another swig of Dussé before the sound of leaves crunching made him look back behind him, where a guy wearing a black and blue Nike Tech and a pair of white, black and blue Air Max 97's stood. The guy stood about five-eight, had dark brown skin and ice blue eyes that sparkled brightly in the moonlight.

"I almost popped yo ass, sneaking up on me and shit," Blake told the man, loosening the grip he had on his Glock 30.

"Bro, if you was one of my opps, you would've been dead," the guy replied with a smirk. Both of them knew he spoke nothing but the truth. Blake was so engulfed in his thoughts that he hadn't even heard him approaching.

"What's the word doe, Blue?" Blake asked Blue, reaching out to shake up with him. He tried shaking up GD with him, but Blue snatched his hand away.

"Dude, I'm not no fuckin GD!" Blue snapped. The smile that quickly replaced his frown eased the tension immediately. "I'm a 4," Blue said, shocking Blake, who just knew for sure Blue had followed the footsteps of his father Willis and his older brother Meechie and became a GD. He never would've thought Blue was a 4Corner Hustler.

"Damn...my bad, Solid," Blake replied with a chuckle. He extended his hand again and this time they shook up 4CH and then GD, showing love to both mobs. He then extended his bottle of Dussé to Blue. He noticed Blue had shed some of his baby fat and had started to grow some stubble under his chin. He was far from the short, chunky, funny kid that was once one of Blake's best friends. A war between Blue's father and Lil Ced's father, Cordale, tore them apart when they were kids.

"You love it up here, don't you?" Blue asked Blake, grabbing the bottle and smacking the rim with four fingers before lifting it to his lips. He passed the bottle back to Blake before taking a seat on the grass not too far from him. This wasn't Blue's first time running into him at the cemetery, his older sister Shana was buried right next to Lil Ced.

They were lovers, who killed themselves over the war that their fathers had going on. They were each other's first and only love and all they desired was to be together peacefully, but their family and friends wouldn't allow it. They tried everything, but they couldn't be together without someone getting hurt. And they loved each other too much to be apart, so they chose to go out on their own terms, which was suicide after a makeshift wedding.

"This the only place where I can really get my mind together," Blake replied before hitting the bottle.

"The streets been talking, and I been hearing about that shit y'all got going on with The Latin Kings. They got half a million on you and two of yo homies," Blue said, pulling out a thick, pre-rolled Backwood stuffed with Gelato. He pulled out a red Bic lighter, flamed up the wood and took a couple heavy pulls. "Yo name hot in the city, everybody tryna get that half-mil," he said after blowing out a lungful of smoke.

"What they saying about me?" Blake asked, not that he really cared what anybody had to say about him, he was just curious as to what kind of dirt was being put on his name. He already knew when you had a name, you became a target for all the haters and wannabes.

"Niggas is scared to fuck with you after hearing how y'all got down on Chito for a load, and then smoked his lil brother. Plus, the nigga Ladale been out here burning everybody, using Cordale's name—"

"We don't fuck with dude!" Blake stated, cutting Blue off. Blue hit the wood a couple more times before responding.

"That part may be true, but everybody knows he's Cordale's brother, so that shit falling back on y'all. And now that the kings been spreading the word about the bag they got on y'all, niggas been whispering about cutting ties with y'all, or back-dooring y'all, whichever one comes first," he said, before handing Blake the wood.

Blake hit the wood and thought about all the shit Blue had just told him, most of it he already knew but the shit about Ladale burning plugs was news to him. He only knew about him burning Chito for about two hundred pounds of exotic and fifty thousand X pills. That was how Blake ended up bumping heads with Chito, who was a high-ranking member of the Latin King nation. Blake was trying to buy a load of exotic weed and X pills from Chito, who told him to come meet with him and do the deal personally. Chito and a gang of his King brothers took the money Ladale owed him, resulting in Cordale's younger cousin, Von D, killing Chito's younger brother.

Blake knew the Kings had initially put a quarter-million on his head as well as Von and KD, but now Blue was saying it was half a million apiece. Blake knew Chito had paper but he didn't imagine his bag being that damn deep. Another thing that was new to Blake was the fact that niggas in the city was scared to fuck with him. He knew Chicago was a cutthroat city, but money ruled the world. He had suspected a few people were staying away from him because of the war and that was understandable, because war slowed down your money a lot.

He had been searching for a consistent plug for months and still hadn't found one, but Aisha had run to Chicago from Memphis with a few million dollars' worth of Percs and Xanax, so that made up for him losing his weed connect. Percocets were the hottest drug in the city and he had real Percs, so he was checking a bag. "How the fuck do you know all this?" he asked before hitting the wood again.

"My brother dead so I had to step up for my pops when he got locked up," Blue replied before taking a swig of Dussé. He originally didn't want to follow his father's footsteps, because he wasn't with all that street shit.

When the war between his father and Cordale first kicked off, it tore him away from Lil Ced, who along with Blake and Six, were Blue's only real friends. They were his best friends, and he took not being able to hang with them hard. He went to school and excelled in sports, up until two bullets to the chest fucked up his sport playing days. He was a casualty of Lil Ced and Shana's sneaking around. Shortly after he got shot, Meechie, who was neck deep in the streets got murdered by Lil Ced, and his father got snatched up by the feds on a drug conspiracy case. So Blue finally accepted his fate and stepped up to run his father's operation.

"Damn, I can remember Lil Ced and Shana telling me you weren't even with that shit," Blake said, not trying to question Blue's gangsta, he was just surprised he was deep in the streets now.

"Shit, I wasn't," Blue said with a shrug and a slight shake of his head. "But that was then, this is now," he added. Blake thought about it for a minute and then remembered that Willis' empire, just like Cordale's, was built off weed. Willis and Cordale came up together off selling weed.

"Y'all got pounds don't y'all?" he asked and Blue nodded. "Aight, what's up? I need a new plug. Y'all got pills, right?"

"I don't got no more X, but I'm loaded on the Percs and Xans. I got that real shit, not them fake ass Percs they got full of fentanyl."

Blue looked at the ground while rubbing the hairs on his chin, adding up the pros and cons of getting money with Blake. It would draw some attention from his peoples, as well as the Latin Kings, but business was business. "I think we could help each other out," he said, nodding his head.

The two friends spoke numbers and delivery while sipping and rotating woods. After discussing business, they reminisced on the past for a while, it actually felt good to both of them being around each other, kickin it how they used to.

It was getting late so Blake decided to leave, he had other shit to attend to. He promised to give Blue a call to work out some more future business ventures.

After leaving the cemetery Blake drove to Hi Five Entertainment's studio in Chicago Heights. He entered studio number four and it looked like it was a fire going on in the room, it was so foggy with exotic smoke. It was a gang of grimy looking niggas and pretty bitches hanging around the room. Some sat on a black sectional couch kicking it while sipping liquor and rotating Backwoods. A few people sat around a wooden table playing spades, and a few more people were scattered around enjoying themselves in some fashion. It looked as if a small party was going on, instead of a studio session.

Molotti stood behind his engineer, C Star, watching him do something on his engineering board. Molotti was shirtless as usual and had on three diamond chains. On one of his Cuban links hung a Double R pendant that resembled the Rolls Royce logo, on one of the other links swung an iced-out 4X pendant. The diamonds in his jewelry danced in the dimly lit room. Molotti wore a bust down Sky Dweller Rolex on his left wrist. His Amiri jeans hung slightly off his ass and sat perfectly on top of his low-top, all-white Air Ones. His small fro was sponged and his razor lining was flawless.

"Play that shit again," he told C Star before turning around to see Blake. He flashed his signature smile and lifted a finger indicating for him to hold on. Seconds later, a nasty beat dropped and a song he had just recorded came on.

Blake nodded his head while listening to the song. The beat was nice, Molotti's flow was on point and watching him rap along to the song like he was performing made Blake like the song even more.

"You dropping the five you takin a risk/Only reason he lit cause the beam on the blick/hoes on my dick can't get tagged in no pic/by no average bitch that's some average shit/I ran it up I can brag on this shit/Spend a bag on my wrist/Hold that bitch in the sky/I'm living good I just hope I don't die/Stand on that business I'm gone need a tie/and we got several switches in this hemi/this fully on full you gone die with that semi/Cut up the Draco let's slide with a mini/One Glock ain't enough so we ridin with plenty. . ."

Molotti rapped, his energy was what made him stand out as a rapper. "That shit decent?" he asked Blake after the song went off.

"Hell yeah, you gotta send me that," Blake replied while shaking up with Molotti, who was a Black P Stone. He was Blake's girlfriend Jala's older brother. He and his fiancée owned an independent record label that was making a lot of noise in the streets. Hi Five Entertainment was as big as it ever was, thanks to Molotti and his homie, Risky Bands, who was also signed to the label. They were receiving offers from a few major labels, but they had a buzz and were doing a great job making their own lane, so they weren't interested in signing with a major. They were real street niggas and were having a hard time adjusting to their rising fame and letting go of their old ways, so Hi Five Entertainment was getting a lot of good and bad publicity.

"You brought that kit for me?" Molotti asked Blake, rubbing his hands together. Instead of responding Blake went into his Dolce bag and pulled out a Ziploc bag containing ten thousand Perc 10's. Molotti's eyes lit up like a bright light. "Aye, Bands!" he called for his homie.

Risky Bands walked over with a small smirk on his face. "Let me see them," Bands mumbled, reaching for the bag of Percs. Bands was a brown-skinned young guy with a low cut, he stood about five-nine and had a birthmark on the right side of his face. He was known in the streets for being a real stepper, even his opps gave him his props.

Blake handed him the bag, he looked at the pills for a second before plucking one out, he threw it in his mouth and swallowed it with a little spit. He was a real Perc head, so it only took him a few seconds to determine the pill was real. "How much you want for these?" he asked, his speech was kind of slurred, due to the fact that he was already high off of three Perc 30s.

"They already bought," Molotti said, reaching for the bag of pills.

"Bro, you don't even pop Percs for real," Bands replied, smacking his lips while holding the Percs out of Molotti's reach. He also wore multiple diamond chains and two of his had big icy 4X pieces hanging from them. The VVS diamonds danced on every one of his pieces. He wore a white and black V Lone t-shirt, a pair of blue Balmain jeans, a pair of wheat Timbs and a white Louie bag to match his white Louis Vuitton belt. He reached in his bag and pulled out a big wad of blue-face hundred-dollar bills.

"Bro, On Stone, you thirsty as hell!" Molotti snapped.

"How much you want for these?" Bands asked Blake, ignoring Molotti.

"Seventy-five thousand," Blake replied with a chuckle. Bands took a seat at the table and started counting out Blake's money, he knew Molotti was only buying the pills just to resell them at a higher price. He, on the other hand, planned on popping the Percs, he was a real addict. It was a drought on real Percs in the city.

"You got another ten thousand?" Molotti asked Blake after snatching a thick wood out of some random chick's hand.

"Yeah, I got a lot of that shit, gang, but I won't be able to get it to you until the morning," Blake replied, causing Molotti to smack his lips.

"Damn, man," he whined. "Aight I'ma need that shit as soon as you get up, bro."

"I'm buying those too," Bands said from the table.

"No, the fuck you not, you hype ass nigga!" Molotti shot back, frowning up his face before turning back to Blake. "Let me holla at you outside gang," he said before grabbing his Glock 31 and putting it on his waist, before pulling an off-white hoodie over his head. They left the studio and Molotti led him to his Hellcat Dodge Durango, it was pearl white with lavender interior.

"This bitch nice," Blake said, complimenting the SUV. Molotti had Double R's stitched in every headrest.

"Good looking, gang. Lavender's my favorite color, it's the uncommon color of royalty. I couldn't ride through the city in a purple ass whip, so I made the inside purple," Molotti explained.

"What's up, doe?" Blake asked. He wasn't trying to be rude, but he knew he hadn't brought him outside just to show off his whip, so he wanted to know what was up.

"You know it's a bag on yo head?" Molotti asked. He didn't have a real friendship with Blake, but his sister was in love with him so that alone was enough for him. He felt obligated to have this conversation with him. Molotti, Bands and a few more of their homies collected money off niggas in the city who had bounties on their heads, and Blake just so happened to pop up on their list. Molotti wanted to let him know. not for his sake, but because he didn't want his sister getting hurt behind whatever Blake had going on in the streets.

"Yeah, you the second mufucka to bring that shit to my attention today," Blake replied, he was doing a good job at hiding the worry he was starting to feel. The Latin Kings must've really been pushing to get him killed.

"This shit for real, gang, and if I know about it, it ain't no telling who else done got wind of it." Molotti paused and took a deep breath before continuing. "Bro, my sister got kidnapped once before and that shit fucked us all up, and I'm sure you know what I did behind that shit. I don't need her getting hurt behind whatever you got going on out here," Molotti paused to fish a half smoked Black & Mild out of his ashtray.

He flamed it up, took a few pulls and continued speaking. "My sisters, they my everything. Jala grown, so I can't tell her to stay away from you, even if I explain to her that you got some niggas on yo ass that really want you dead. She not gone see it as me wanting to keep her safe, she only gone see it as her big brother being overprotective." He paused again, trying to think of the best way to word how he was feeling. "If something happen to sis, it's gone get ugly for everybody involved, On Stone," he stated, not hiding the threat behind his words.

Blake bit the inside of his jaw, he wanted to check him but at the same time, he understood where he was coming from, if he had a younger sister, he would feel the same way. "She good, bro," he replied dryly.

"You saying that shit now, but them niggas not gone give you a pass just because you with her. If they catch you and she with you, they gone try they luck, they not gone give a fuck if she get hit or not," Molotti shot back. Jala was his youngest sister and even though he was closer to his twin sister, Big T, he couldn't deny Jala was his favorite. He adored her in every way. He knew she wouldn't listen to his advice if he was to tell her to keep her distance from Blake. She didn't understand street politics, so he said fuck it and went straight to Blake. He was hoping that a man-to-man conversation would help Blake see things his way.

"I feel where you coming from, gang, and I'ma do everything in my power to keep her safe and out of harm's way."

"Please and thank you," Molotti said, flashing his signature smile. "You know this bitch bulletproof?" he asked, referring to his Durango.

"Yeah?" Blake asked, faking interest.

"Yes, sirski!" Molotti chuckled. He had a lot of opps and was worth big points. If he were to get caught lacking, he wasn't going out like that, though he was always on point. "I been thinking about taking the tints off this bitch so niggas can see me out in traffic, not worried 'bout a damn thing."

"Naw, don't do that," Blake suggested with a chuckle.

"What's the point of having this shit if I can't show it off?" Molotti asked. "I remember when we was riding steamers, praying we didn't get them bitches bumped off. Now, me and all my niggas riding foreign and luxury vehicles. I deserve to rub this shit in the mufuckas' faces who didn't believe in me, don't I?"

Blake was sitting there with a confused look on his face. It seemed like Molotti needed someone to vent to but considering the fact that the two had never chopped it up on such a deep level, Blake didn't know how to respond. "Ain't no question," he finally agreed before yawning and stretching his long body. "I'm 'bout to get up outta here. I'll have them pills ready for you first thing in the morning," he said then shook up with Molotti before getting out of the SUV.

Molotti also climbed out and started heading back to the studio. "Aye, Blake!" he called out before Blake was all the way into his car. "Stay dangerous!" he yelled and entered the studio.

After leaving the studio, Blake went straight to the Cambria Hotel, where he had been staying for the past week. It was late, so he expected for Aisha to be asleep, but she wasn't. She was sitting on the queen-sized bed, scrolling through her *IG* timeline. "Hey Stink," she greeted Blake with a smile, showing her deep dimples and pretty white teeth. She had her long, thick hair pulled into a big, puffy ponytail. The dark bags under her eyes showed she had been stressing lately.

"What's up, bae?" Blake asked after giving her a kiss on the lips.

"Nothing, I was waiting on you to make it back," she replied. She knew there was money on his head, so anytime he left out, she would be on edge until he returned. She wasn't only worried about the Latin kings catching up with him, she had a few men from Memphis in the city looking for her.

Her ex-boyfriend Domo, and his father Lumps were getting money in South Memphis, and after they hit a huge lick on a lot of Percocets, Xanax and Viagras, Aisha robbed them and fled to Chicago. Domo and Lumps had already murdered her mother and auntie, who she'd left back in Memphis without telling them what she did. Now, the two men were in Chicago hunting her down. They didn't know Blake and they didn't know where she was, but just knowing they were on her trail in the city made her very paranoid.

When Aisha ran to Chicago, she didn't know anyone, not even her father Cordale. They met through a jail visit and clicked immediately. Cordale asked Blake to take Aisha in until she got comfortable, and everything was all well until they fell in love. Aisha was with Blake's right-hand man KD at first. He was head over heels in love with her, but his insecure ways pushed her right into Blake's arms.

They did an okay job at hiding what they had going on, until Aisha pocket-dialed KD, and he overheard them confessing their love for one another before having sex. That was the straw that broke the camel's back for KD, he declared Blake a snake and let him know it was up whenever they crossed paths. So far, they hadn't run across each other, and Blake was grateful for that, because the last thing he wanted to do was kill his boy over a piece of pussy that belonged to neither one of them.

"I bagged up all the Percs by the thousands," Aisha told Blake as he took a seat on the bed next to her.

"You must've been in this bitch bored as hell," Blake replied with a chuckle.

"Sure was."

"I needed to do that anyway, so thank you."

"KD texted me earlier."

"And said what?"

"He told me to be safe," Aisha said, going to their text message thread and showing it to Blake. Blake noticed KD had told Aisha he still was in love with her. She didn't respond but he noticed she *loved* the message. If he was feeling any type of way about it he did a good job at holding his composure and hiding it. The fact that KD was sending a subliminal threat through Aisha had him upset. That was his shit. If it was on, then it was on, and it wasn't shit to talk about. Before he could respond, his phone started ringing, it was Von D.

"What's the word, gang?" he answered.

"What's the word, my boy? Where you at?" Von D asked, he had a Risky Bands song playing loudly in the background.

"I'm in traffic on my way to buss this swerve," Blake lied quickly. Von D was Aisha's younger cousin and even though he was locked in with Blake he also fucked with KD tough. And with all the bullshit going on, Blake didn't truly know if he could trust him or not.

"You got some Percs on you?" Von D asked, turning down his music.

"Yeah, how many you need?"

"A thousand."

"Aight, meet me at the Shell gas station on 79th and State."

"Bet," Von D replied before hanging up.

"Can I ride with you?" Aisha asked Blake before handing him a Ziploc bag full of Perc 30s. She had been waiting for him to come in for hours, and not even a full ten minutes after he finally came in, he was on his way back out. She craved some of his time and attention.

"Yeah, if you want to," Blake said. Aisha quickly got up and slid on a pair of Chanel jogging pants. The small smile on her face showed how excited she was. It was something about him that made her feel like a little girl. She got butterflies every time she was in his presence.

Blake tried his best to disguise it but deep down he felt the exact same way about her. The only problem was Jala, who he was also deeply in love with. He was torn between the two. At the moment, he just didn't love Aisha enough to walk away from his relationship with Jala. It was complicated being in love with two women at the same time and the fact that they both seemed to be perfect for him, only made it harder for him and his poor heart.

Once inside Blake's new Benz, Aisha hooked her phone up to the car's Bluetooth and went to her favorite Summer Walker song. "This yo shit, ain't it?" Blake asked, flaming up a half-smoked wood stuffed with exotic weed.

"Only because she saying everything I want to say to you," Aisha replied.

"You know what song make me think of you?"

"Which one?"

Instead of responding, Blake grabbed her phone and went to "All This Love" by Trey Songz. Aisha's dark skin flushed as he started singing to her. He wasn't a good singer at all, but to her it was the thought that counted.

"You are so silly," She giggled, grabbing the wood that he was handing her.

"Let's have four or five pretty ass daughters," he said.

"I don't want all girls. I want a couple of sons."

"Yeah, that'll be cool, we can have two sons and name them Cragg and Cedric."

"That sounds like a plan I think we should start working on that tonight," Aisha said, leaning over and licking Blake's cheek. He loved when she did freaky shit like that.

"You better stop playing before I pull this mufucka over and do something to you," he warned Aisha, who ignored his threat and unbuckled his Louis Vuitton belt, before unbuckling his Amiri jeans and pulling out his soft dick, she slid it into her warm mouth and began to give him head. He let his seat back a little and got comfortable while she did her shit. Once he was fully erect, she started sucking like her life depended on it.

Blake got off the E-way on 79th and parked his car on 79th and Wabash. He let his seat all the way back and grabbed the back of Aisha's head, forcing his dick all the way down her throat. He used his other hand to reach over and start pulling her pants off. She wasn't wearing any panties, so once they were off, he stuck his middle finger inside her tight, wet pussy. She moaned in ecstasy while he finger-fucked her. Aisha's pussy was throbbing and sucking his finger in like a vacuum. He loved how wet she got, and her natural body fragrance was turning him on more and more.

"Come here," he told her, taking his finger out of her pussy and lightly smacking her ass. Aisha quickly spit his dick out of her mouth and hurriedly climbed on top of him. She slowly slid down on his wet dick. He grabbed two handfuls of ass and held on while she rode him.

"I...love...youuu," Aisha moaned before giving him a kiss on the lips. She slipped her tongue into his mouth and tongue wrestled with him for a second. "Fuck!" she gasped, feeling his dick in her stomach. It didn't take long for him to make her cum all over his dick. When he felt her vaginal walls clenching, he knew she was having an orgasm, so he held her up and sped up his strokes. "Shit! Shit! Shit!" Aisha squealed as Blake beat her pussy up.

Blake felt his nut coming but he wasn't ready to bust just yet so he abruptly stopped, pulled Aisha off his dick, and told her to climb into the backseat. After lifting both of the seats up as far as they could go, he climbed in the back with her. He laid her on the backseat and got down on his knees to eat her pussy. He viciously attacked her clitty with his tongue. He knew exactly how she liked her pussy eaten, so he sucked and nibbled on her clit, while rubbing her asshole with his thumb. After a while he slid his thumb in her tight asshole while eating her pussy, that drove her crazy, making her cum again.

After ten minutes of eating pussy, Blake got between Aisha's legs and put her feet in the air and started pounding her out. She was moaning and whining, sounding like a wounded animal. "Play with that pussy for daddy," Blake demanded, and she immediately started rubbing her clit while he fucked her.

"Oh…my…God!" she screamed and started squirting all over his dick. He pulled out and smacked her clit with his rock-hard head. He then rubbed his head up and down her opening, before sliding back in and continuing his assault on her pussy.

Blake grabbed one of Aisha's small feet and started planting soft kisses all over the bottom of it, while slowly sliding in and out of her. After a few kisses he started sucking on her big toe. He sucked each toe individually before switching to the other foot. Aisha had some of the prettiest toes he'd ever seen and he made it his duty to show her feet some love during sex He kept one of her toes in his mouth and picked up the pace of his strokes.

He looked down to see his dick painted white with the cream from her pussy. He loved the fact that she was a squirter and a creamer, plus the fact that her pussy was tight made her one of the best sex partners he ever experienced. Her angelic moans were what pushed him over the edge, he busted a huge nut inside of her and collapsed on top of her, breathing heavily.

"I needed that," Aisha told Blake before leaning forward and giving him a kiss. That one kiss turned into a longer, more passionate round of tongue kissing and in a matter of minutes, Blake's dick was back rock hard. As soon as he slid inside of her, his phone started ringing.

"Yoooo," he answered for Von D.

"How far are you?" Von D asked.

"I'ma be pulling up in three minutes."

"Bet," Von D replied before hanging up.

Blake and Aisha reluctantly got dressed. They both wanted to go another round but business before pleasure was a rule. The gas station Blake was meeting Von D at was on the next block. So, after quickly getting dressed, he pulled into the gas station's parking lot and parked his car next to Von D's black 392 Dodge Charger.

Von D hopped out of his car and jumped in Blake's backseat. "It smell like sex in this bitch," he said, scrunching up his face. "Y'all was just fucking?" he asked, making Aisha erupt in laughter.

"Naw, man," Blake lied with a chuckle. He grabbed the Ziploc bag full of Percs out of his armrest and handed them to Von.

"What I owe you?" Von D asked, pulling a wad of blue-face hundreds out of his pocket.

"Fifteen thousand," Blake replied while unraveling a Backwood.

"Fasho," Von D said before turning to Aisha. "What's up with you, cuz? You good?" he asked while counting out Blake's money.

"Hey, cuz, I'm doing fine."

"Yo country ass, when you gone invite some of them Memphis hoes down here, so we can show them how we comin in the Raq?"

"You don't need no more hoes, lil cuz."

Why you say that?" Von D asked, taking a break from counting the money to look at Aisha like she was crazy.

"Because I been up here for a while now, and I still haven't seen you with the same woman on more than one occasion. You a lil bop."

"You know what you know, cuz," Von D said with a chuckle and got back to counting. "I need some Xans, too, gang. The fiends I be dumping always asking for Xans," he told Blake.

"I got green and yellow bars, you can give me twenty-five hundred for a thousand of 'em," Blake replied before pausing to flame up his wood. "You still fucking with that dog food, huh?" he asked after exhaling a lung full of smoke. Von D, along with KD had invested in a few keys of heroin, even though Blake and Cordale were against selling dope. Ever since they'd started selling dope, Von D and KD had completely given up selling weed and X pills. The money they were making off dope was coming in four times faster than the money they were seeing selling weed.

"Hell yeah, I'm not gone lie. That paper be coming in so fast sometimes, it be scaring me. You need to stop playing and come get some of this money."

"I know you heard the saying, 'If it ain't broke don't fix it'." Blake paused to hit the wood a few times before handing it to Aisha and continuing. "I got enough prescription pills to keep me situated for a long, long time. That dope money good, but I'm straight. I'ma stay in my lane," he said. Cordale had put it in his head a long time ago that heroin attracted the feds and it was no telling if he was already on the fed's radar or not, considering the fact that he'd been working under Cordale for years now.

"So that shit KD been talkin' about must be true?" Von D asked.

Blake looked at him through the rearview mirror. "What he saying?" he asked. His hand crept towards his lap where his Glock sat. He didn't know what Von D was on and just in case he was on some bullshit, Blake was ready to take his ass out.

"He keep yelling you and Aisha hit a big lick behind our backs."

"On my brother grave, that lame ass nigga don't know what the fuck he talkin' about. Aisha hit a lick in Memphis on her own. I didn't even know shit about what she had going on until recently," Blake told Von D, still glaring at him through the rearview.

"He said y'all fucking too. What's to that?" Von D asked and the dumb look on Blake's face confirmed that at least that rumor was true. That explained the sex in the air when he climbed in the car the two freaks were fresh off a sex session.

"Yeah, we are," Blake admitted for the first time. He took his eyes off the rearview mirror. He knew he was wrong and couldn't stand to look at Von D in his eyes. It got awkwardly silent for a brief second before Von D spoke.

"My dawg really in his feelings about that shit, On Stone," he said, grabbing the wood Aisha was handing him. He hit the wood a few times and continued speaking. "You know I'ma keep it a buck with you, gang. You and I both know you foul for fucking on cuz when you knew that folks was in love with her." Blake nodded his head in agreement. "It ain't shit you could tell me to justify that shit, but I keep telling KD it's not that serious, to where he wanna kill you," he said before hitting the wood again.

"That's what he saying he wanna do, huh?"

"Yeah, folks really wanna do something to you," Von D replied honestly.

Blake took a deep breath. He knew if nobody else knew what was going through KD's head, Von did. Blake knew KD, so he knew if he had his mind set on it being smoke between them, then it would be just that whenever they bumped heads. He had too much other shit going on to be beefing with his closest friend.

"What's up with that location you was supposed to have for me?" Blake asked, subtly changing the subject.

"I'm 'bout to send it to you right now," Von D said. His homie Nutso was able to provide him the address of one of the Latin Kings named Pookie.

"You know they upped the price they got on us?"

"Naw, this my first time hearing that. How much they got on us now?"

"Half a million apiece." Von D whistled before a nervous chuckle escaped his lips. A half a million dollars was enough to make the best of friends turn on one another.

"Damn, them corn-eating mufuckas really tryna get us out the way, huh?"

"Hell yeah, and they letting the whole city know, so it ain't no telling who might be on our ass." Von D was a gangsta by all means, but hearing it was a half a million dollars on his head changed his whole vibe. He could already feel his paranoia starting to kick in. "On Stone, we gotta figure this shit out, our money long but it ain't long enough to keep warring with King nem."

"You right. We'll figure it out, doe. just let KD know to keep his eyes open," Blake said, causing Von D to subtly frown up. "Not for me, for the Kings," Blake said, after picking up on the look.

"Aight, man. Stay dangerous, gang," Von D said, opening the car door to get out.

"You too, gang," Blake replied.

Chapter 2

The rays of sun danced off Blake's diamond Cuban link, he should've left it in the car, but he was in such a rush it slipped his mind. He was in one of the Latin Kings named Pookie's backyard hiding behind a big bush, his homie Knuckles was so close behind him, he could feel the heat from his breath on the back of his neck. They were looking through Pookie's kitchen window, watching him argue with a beautiful Latino woman.

"Fuck it, let's go," Blake told Knuckles, who crouched down and led the way to Pookie's back door. Knuckles lifted his leg and kicked the doorknob with his black Timbs, knocking it open on his first kick. Pookie was so startled, for a few seconds he stood there frozen in shock. The first thing he saw was Knuckle's Tech. Knuckles squeezed the trigger, hitting Pookie in his chest and shoulder twisting his lean body.

Blake lifted his Micro Draco and sent a volley of 7.62 shells towards Pookie and his bitch, only for Knuckles to step in his line of fire and catch a 7.62 shell to the back of his bald head, bursting it open like a cantaloupe. Blood and brain matter splashed all over Blake's face. He wiped blood from his eyes to see Pookie's bitch stretched over their marble island bleeding from a gaping hole in her neck.

Pookie, on the other hand, was hightailing it towards the living room, trying to make it to the front door. Blake bolted after him, cradling the Draco with two hands. He squeezed the trigger, trying to hit Pookie before he could make it to the door. Pookie made it to the door without getting shot and would've made it out the door, if he hadn't had to tussle with all the locks he had on the front door. By the time he unlocked the first bolt and took the chain off the second lock, Blake was a few steps behind him with his Draco. He squeezed the trigger, and the 7.62 shells tore through Pookie's body with ease and through the wooden door.

Blake stood over Pookie and put two bullets in his head to make sure he wasn't getting back up. He immediately rushed to the kitchen to check on Knuckles. He knew for a fact he was dead, but he wanted to make sure. Once back in the kitchen, it only took one glance to confirm his friend was long gone. Blake shook his head and crossed his chest before stepping over Knuckle's body and jetting out of the back door.

"Fuck!" he gruffed once inside the striker plated SRT Dodge Challenger he had bought specifically for the mission. Once he pulled off, he *FaceTimed* his homie Lil Moe, one of the Black P Stones from Eight Trey Mob.

"What's the word, gang?" Lil Moe asked after blowing a cloud of exotic smoke towards the camera.

"Man, Knuckles dead," Blake said sadly. A few tears fell from his eyes.

"What the fuck happened?" Lil Moe asked sullenly. Knuckles had made a name for himself as being a stepper, and Lil Moe had made his name doing the same shit he watched Knuckles do. They weren't everyday niggas but the two were very close, so the news saddened him.

"We got the drop on one of the Kings, so we kicked in his door and the dumb ass nigga jumped in front of me while I was blowing the Drac," Blake explained.

"Damn, that shit crazy," Lil Moe said, shaking his head and wiping a few tears from his face. "Where you at now?" he asked.

"I'm 'bout to go change whips."

"Aight, pull up on me in the hood after you change whips."

"Aight," Blake said and hung up.

Thirty minutes later, he was pulling up on 79th and Evans in his BMW X5. Men and women were scattered up and down the block, some were hustling, some were out just enjoying the good weather. It was an unusually warm November day and niggas was outside like it was the middle of July. Blake parked, put his Glock on his waist and hopped out. He approached Lil Moe, who was standing amongst a crowd of men and women who were talking shit and rotating Backwoods.

"What's the word, Law?" Blake asked Lil Moe, reaching out to shake up with him. They were from the same hood, despite them being in different gangs. At one point in time, it was unusual to see members of different gangs all claiming the same hood. It would normally be all GD's or all Vice Lords, but nowadays it was more about where you were from, and not what gang you claimed. In certain areas of the city, Black Stones were clicked up with GD's, or 4Corner Hustlers were clicked up with BD's, and into it with other Vice Lords. You even had some hoods that consisted of three different gangs. Chicago was past gangbanging. The city was clique banging now.

"I was just telling folks about the time when me and Knuckles got in that high speed on 87th and folk's goofy ass crashed before we could even make it to the E-way." Lil Moe chuckled and even though everyone was in a somber mood, a few people laughed at the memory.

"Knuckles shitted on his self that day, didn't he?" Blake asked before erupting in laughter. He was laughing so hard his stomach started hurting.

"On Lil Ced grave, I was laughing so hard I couldn't even run," Lil Moe said.

They continued to trade stories about Knuckles until KD walked up, followed by a few of the older folks. He had a frown on his face and negative energy radiated from him. "What happened to Knuckles?" he asked Lil Moe, not caring to mask the attitude in his tone.

"Ask folks, he was with him," Lil Moe said, nodding towards Blake, who was standing there with a smug expression on his face. Lil Moe knew at the moment they weren't seeing eye to eye, but Blake was the one who killed Knuckles, so he thought it would be best if he let him explain what happened on his own.

"So, what happened?" KD gruffed.

Blake's initial reaction was to check KD for the way he was talking to him, but instead he let it slide and said, "We ran in one of the King's crib and folks jumped in front of me while I was blowing the Drac."

"So, you killed bro on a hit?" KD asked with disbelief written all over his face.

"Basically," Blake replied dryly.

"On Lil Ced grave, if that ain't the goofiest shit ever, I don't know what is," he said with a chuckle. "I'm not even surprised doe."

"And what that supposed to mean?"

The tension was building quickly and the ones who knew Blake and KD were beefing were watching, anxious to see what type of bullshit unfolded. KD had been woofin everyday about what he was going to do to Blake when he caught him and now, they were face to face, so everyone was waiting to see if KD was going to walk it like he talked it.

"It means exactly what I said, you killing Knuckles on a hit was some goofy shit. On Lil Ced grave, it ain't no way around that, and I'm not surprised because I know you a goofy ass nigga," KD replied, not breaking eye contact with Blake.

"Don't get fucked up by this goofy," Blake spat angrily. He was trying his best to control his anger, but it was no way he would let KD, or any other nigga disrespect him.

"You not even like that, for real," KD said, waving him off.

"Try me and see."

"I should be getting on yo ass anyway, you lucky folks nem telling me to let you breathe."

That made Blake laugh. "KD, stop playin with me," he warned.

"On Lil Ced, I'm not playin' at all," KD shot back with a mug. His hand slid near his waistline and that's when Blake upped his Glock, he didn't aim it at KD, but he had it out and was ready to use it. "Fuck you gone do with that?" KD asked, upping his Glock. The crowd quickly started to disperse. Nobody wanted to catch a stray bullet.

Blake started to backpedal to his car, the look in KD's eyes told him he was ready to blow, so he did what any other nigga would do and started blowing first. KD immediately returned fire and everyone that was out there started running, screaming and ducking trying to avoid catching a stray bullet.

The sixteen shots Blake had in his clip were gone quickly and KD was still shooting. Blake hopped in his car and peeled off. He almost hit a little girl who was running across the street, but he slammed his foot on the brake and skidded to a stop. The little girl took off and Blake sped off just as another gun went off.

***

When Blake pulled up in front of the house he had just rented in Aisha's name, he got out and checked his car to see multiple bullet holes in it. He was mad, but he'd most rather have bullet holes in his car than in his body. He shook his head, sighed and went into the house.

When he walked in, the smell of freshly fried chicken attacked his nostrils, his stomach growled, reminding him he hadn't eaten anything all day. The living room was empty and made the house look vacant. Inside the kitchen, Aisha stood over the stove frying chicken. The kitchen had a wooden table with two chairs. Blake had only moved a few of his possessions in the home, but he planned on paying a few hypes to move all his belongings into the house whenever he had some free time.

When Aisha turned around and saw Blake, she smiled and said, "Hey, Stink." Blake walked up, gave her a hug and a peck on the lips before surveying the pots and pans on the stove. His mouth started to water looking at the pot of dirty rice she was stirring.

"That shit smell good as hell," he told her, planting a kiss on the nape of her neck. Before she could respond, his phone went off. It was a *FaceTime* from Lil Moe. "What's up?" Blake answered. He knew it was some bullshit because Lil Moe's eyes were red and puffy from crying, and his face was still wet with tears.

"Why the fuck did you have to start shooting, gang?" Lil Moe asked.

"That nigga acted like he was about to blick me down, so I had to do what I had to do," Blake said defensively. "What happened, doe?" he asked.

"My pops got hit in his head," Lil Moe replied. His pops, Man, was one of the older folks from the hood. Blake didn't know how to respond to the news at first.

After a few seconds of silence, he finally said, "Damn, is he straight?"

"It wasn't looking good," Lil Moe said, shaking his head. "So, I left the hospital."

"Damn bro, I'm sorry to hear that shit," Blake said sincerely.

He was standing behind KD," Lil Moe said, and that's when Blake realized he was only calling him to point the finger at him. The last thing he needed was for another one of his guys to have a reason to feel some type of way about him.

"So, you tryna say I did that shit?"

"You was the only one shooting in that direction, so it had to be you."

"Even if it was me, bro, you know that shit wasn't intentional."

"You saying that, but yo name been involved in a lot of funny shit, it's like you on some backdoor shit with all the guys." Lil Moe's last comment caught Blake completely off guard. He knew for a fact that some of his homies were whispering about him, putting dirt on his name, trying to tarnish his reputation. Most likely, KD was the main one.

"On my brother, I haven't back doored none of my niggas, so what the fuck is you talkin' about?" Blake asked, mugging the camera.

"Nigga, you back doored Lil Ced," Lil Moe growled. "Nigga KD told me how you told Ladale all type of shit about Lil Ced, and that's what made him put that money on folk's head," Lil Moe added.

Blake knew exactly what he was talking about. After he kidnapped Millie and Lil Ced helped her get away, he told Ladale all of Lil Ced's secrets and that led to Lil Ced being outcast from the hood. Ladale had also put some money on his head, and Lil Moe was one of the ones who had tried to collect it but failed. KD had recently convinced him Blake was hatin' on Lil Ced, so he manipulated the whole situation.

"On my brother, you sound dumb as hell," Blake snapped. "You letting bitch ass niggas feed you lies. Don't fall for that shit, cause I'm telling you it's not gone end well."

"What that supposed to mean?"

"Take it how you wanna take it," Blake said.

"Say less," Lil Moe said and hung up.

Aisha stood there staring at Blake trying to figure out what had just happened. Blake, on the other hand, was able to see the play for what it was. Lil Moe was using his father's getting shot in the head as an excuse to take KD's side, and ride against him. Man wasn't even Lil Moe's biological father. KD had manipulated Lil Moe to believe Blake had shot Man on purpose. Blake wasn't surprised at all, he knew Lil Moe would side with KD over him, he just hoped it'd never get to that point. KD and Lil Moe had a lot of influence over the younger guys from the hood, so Blake knew he had to be careful with who he fucked with.

His boy Suemoo was out of the hospital but still in the recovery stage. He wasn't in Blake's circle for real, but he was one person he knew he could count on at the moment.

The next few days Blake tried moving like a ghost, his paranoia was turned up to the max and he was moving with extreme caution. He refused to get up with any of the guys and steered clear of the hood altogether. He wasn't sure who all KD had riding with him and until he knew for sure, he would stay away from everybody.

Blake and Blue had finally found the time to get up together and lock in a business deal. Blake knew with all the pills he had, and the weed Blue had, they would run their bag to the next level. Blue supplied him with two hundred pounds of twenty different strains of exotic weed. The only problem was that Blake couldn't get money in his hood, so he needed somewhere else to dump his pounds at.

That's where Von D came into play, wasn't no weed on his block in the Hundreds, and he had a few homies that wouldn't mind opening up shop. He introduced Blake to Boothie Bucks and Wet Em Up. Boothie Bucks was an up-and-coming rapper who was just recently released from prison. He wasn't much of a hustler, he was more of a finesser, but if you dropped fifty pounds on him, he would be able to get them off. Wet Em Up was one of Von D's closest friends, a hot head that lived solely for putting in work. He dibbled and dabbled in fraud to keep himself dressed in designer, with pockets full of money.

Blake gave Boothie and Wet Em Up fifty pounds that they trapped out of a two-flat on 106th and Indiana. After a couple of weeks, the trap was starting to make some noise, so Blake decided to let them sell Percs and Xans out of the trap too. He was giving Von D a percentage of the trap's weekly profit, not just because Von had given him an avenue to make some money in his hood, but he was also trying to win Von over. He knew that he couldn't war against his block and the Latin Kings on his own, so he needed some type of backup.

Blake started spending a lot of time in the 106th trap; at first, he didn't too much care for Boothie. He thought he was too loud and sought the wrong kind of attention. Blake clicked with Wet Em Up instantly and it was genuine. He had heard stories of the bodies Wet had caught but after being around him, you wouldn't have expected him to be the coldblooded killer the streets made him out to be. He was very quiet and observing. He would sit in the trap dumping off his phone all day, while Boothie wrote raps and told over-exaggerated war stories.

It took a few days for Wet Em Up to feel Blake out but once he did, he noticed they had a lot in common. All of Von D's guys knew Jala, so by Blake being her boyfriend he was good by association.

While Blake was adjusting to making money in the Hundreds, Aisha was loving the role as stay-at-home girlfriend she was playing. Jala was still in the picture, but that didn't matter to her, because she got way more of Blake's time than Jala did. The love she had for Blake had her mind gone, everything she did, she did for him. She knew he was business minded, so she had been taking online real estate courses and was looking to purchase some property. Blake wasn't into real estate but his brother Six was, so he was willing to get involved.

Blake couldn't deny he was in love with Aisha. She was the perfect woman for him, she cooked, she cleaned, she catered to his every want and need, plus she had put him in a position to take his bag to the next level. He truly appreciated her for that.

Their only problem was the nigga Domo, who was in the city, searching for Aisha. He was like a ghost because neither of them knew where he was or who he was connected to. Blake wished he knew where to start looking for him because the quicker he killed him, the quicker he could have Aisha feeling safe and secure. Patience would be the key. Sooner or later, Domo would have to show his face.

***

The vibrating of his phone woke Blake up from a light slumber, he had just recently dozed off. He grabbed his phone and answered the *FaceTime* call, he looked at the screen to see Blue cheesing into the camera. "You sleep, nigga?" Blue asked.

"I had just dozed off," Blake said, wiping crust from his eyes. "What's the word doe, gang?"

"I'm tryna kick it, gang, let's go out somewhere," Blue replied before taking a hit off a wood he was holding and blowing the smoke at the camera.

Blake was hesitant, just based on the history he had with Blue's family. Blue's brother murdered his brother, he'd kidnapped Blue's sister and even though Blue never got involved, they were just from two different sides of the field. Cordale and Willis had squashed their beef, but Blake still didn't fuck with the niggas from 47th and them niggas didn't fuck with him.

"Where you tryna pop out to?" Blake asked, yawning.

"Let's go to Club O or something,"

"Hell naw," Blake frowned. "I don't really fuck with the clubs like that, especially not the ones that everybody be going to."

Blue thought for a second before suggesting, "My lil bitch having a girls' night with a bunch of her buddies, we can crash that bitch."

"Hell naw, man, you on some bullshit," Blake said with a chuckle. He was really leery of Blue, they were doing good business together, but that was about it.

"On my brother, we good. She ain't gone trip and all her friends bad as hell," Blue said. He must've sensed Blake's suspicion because he smiled and said, "On my brother and sister's grave, I'm not on no funny shit. I'm just tryna catch up with my old friend and have a good time."

Blake thought about it for a second. "What time?" he asked reluctantly. He had no reason to trust Blue but at the same time, something in his soul told him everything would be ok. That, plus he knew he would shoot himself out of any situation.

"Be ready by like eleven."

"Aight bet," Blake said before hanging up.

After getting off the phone, Blake decided to slide through the Hundreds and fuck with Wet Em Up. He pulled in front of the 106th trap to see Wet Em Up and a few of his guys sitting on the front porch. He honked his horn and Wet Em Up got up and trotted to his car.

"What's the word, G?" he asked, leaning in the passenger's window. His black and white Moncler bubble coat concealed the Glock 22 he had on his waistline. His dreads were freshly twisted, and they hung just below his shoulders.

"Shit, what you on, my boy?" Blake asked, popping the locks so he could get in the car.

"Getting this shit off, you know what time it is."

"You feel like riding with me real quick?"

"It don't matter."

A few minutes later, Blake was pulling up in front of an abandoned crib on 113th street and made a call. "Roll up," he told Wet Em Up, nodding towards an ounce of Birthday Cake and a pack of Russian Cream Backwoods that sat in the cupholder. "You know P Ball, don't you?" Blake asked him.

"Hell yeah," Wet Em Up replied with a nod. That made Blake feel a little bit better, he figured having Wet Em Up with him would keep P Ball honest. He was meeting him to give him fifty thousand but before giving him the money, P Ball had to prove to him he was holding up to his side of the agreement.

Halfway through their wood, P Ball pulled up in a Gray Infiniti Q7 and hopped out with his signature smirk on his face. Blake and Wet Em Up both hopped out and met him at the back of his truck.

"Wet Em Up, what's the word, gang?" P Ball asked, greeting him with a shake. "Let me find out Von D done flipped you, D Block," he said, turning to Blake.

"He an honorary member," Wet Em Up joked.

"We locked in for real you know how that shit go," Blake said, pulling the hood to his gray Moose Knuckle coat over his head. "Let's get this shit out the way, doe."

P Ball smirked and led them into an abandoned house. The inside of the house was rank and smelled like mildew. The living room was empty, except for a musty, dingy red couch and a battered card table. It was dark in the house but the flashlight on P Ball's iPhone gave them enough light to maneuver through the house. The basement was darker than the rest of the house and smelled more rancid.

P Ball aimed the light towards the corner of the room, where a man sat tied in a chair. The man's hair was nappy, and his beard was unkempt, he looked like a homeless bum. His lips were swollen and one of his eyes was black. He lifted his head and squinted his eyes, trying to see who was behind the light. Blake pulled out his iPhone and turned on his flashlight and illuminated himself. The man in the chair eyes grew large when he locked eyes with Blake, who shot him a wicked grin. "What's up, Unc?" Blake asked him.

"Finally," the man mumbled. Blake even thought he saw the corners of the man's mouth threaten to curl upward into a smile.

"Finally, what?"

"Finally, I can die and get this shit over with. Fuck took you so long?"

"It look like somebody done told you wrong," Blake replied with a chuckle. He laughed even harder when the man's face dropped, showing his disappointment.

The man was Ladale, Cordale's older brother. He was the man who started the war between Cordale and Willis. The same war that cost Blake's brother his life. Blake hated Ladale, not only was he a hoe ass nigga, he was also a federal informant. P Ball was able to snatch him up and hold him for Blake.

Blake needed to see him in person to confirm it. "It's not yo time yet," Blake told Ladale.

"Fuck you," Ladale roared and spit towards Blake but missed him. "You always been a lil pussy, you and yo brother," he growled. He had been confined to that dark basement for Lord only knows how long, he got fed three sometimes four times a day and somebody came to let him shower every few days. He spent all day sitting in that chair, kicking away rats and singing songs to himself. He didn't know whether it was night or day. He felt like he was losing his mind.

Many times, he tried to get P Ball or one of his homies to kill him and take him out his misery. He knew he was going to die sooner or later. They weren't holding him for nothing but to him, later felt like it was taking an eternity to come. He knew his chances of escaping were close to none. He was like a prisoner on death row, waiting on his turn to ride the chair.

"What the fuck y'all got going on?" Wet Em Up asked laughing. His laugh was more out of nervousness than anything else. He was a killer but to see that P Ball and Blake had a nigga tied up was something he'd never seen before.

"This nigga a rat and he crossed the wrong niggas," Blake said grimly, looking Ladale in his beady rat eyes. Ladale didn't break his gaze.

"I'll make sure to tell Six and Lil Ced you send your regards," he said and with the quickness of a cat, Blake had the barrel of his Glock pressed into his forehead.

"You just don't know how bad I wanna shoot yo fuckin face off," he said through clenched jaws. His finger caressed the trigger. He wanted to pull it so badly, but he had bigger plans for Ladale, so he just smacked him across the forehead with the gun opening him up.

"Arghhh!" Ladale bellowed in pain.

"Soon Ladale," Blake promised, turning off his flashlight. "Soon you gone get everything you got coming," he said, before leaving out the basement.

***

Later that night, Blake and Wet Em Up were following Blue to his girlfriend's house in Hoffman Estates. Blake had talked Blue into letting Wet Em Up tag along, he felt secure with an extra set of eyes with him. He gave Wet Em Up a brief rundown on his history and relationship with Blue, just so he wouldn't be in the blind. The house they pulled up to was a huge one that looked like it belonged to a politician or something.

"Damn this yo bitch crib?" Blake asked Blue once they were out of their cars.

"Hell yeah," Blue replied cooly with a small smile. When they entered the home, he led them to the huge living room, where a bunch of women wearing onesies were shaking ass to Pop Smoke's, "She Got a Thing."

"Ayeeee!" Blake said doing a little two-step with a smile on his face. Every woman in the room was gorgeous to say the least. Even the ugliest one was beautiful.

He watched Blue run up on a petite, light-skinned woman with long curly hair, she had to be mixed with something. He started smacking her ass while she twerked. When the song went off, she gave Blue a tight hug and a juicy kiss on his lips.

Blake looked around the room and caught a few women eyeballing him. He wore a gray Moose Knuckle coat with the white fur around the hood, a white Amiri t-shirt that said AMIRI in gray letters, a pair of light blue Amiri skinny jeans and a pair of gray Timbs. Wet Em Up, was also getting his fair share of looks and smiles. Wet wore his white and black bubble Moncler coat, a black Moncler skullcap over his dreads, a white and black Dior t-shirt, a pair of black PURPLE jeans and a pair of crispy, all-white low-top Air Ones.

"Baby, this my homie, Blake I was telling you about," Blue said, nodding towards Blake. "And that's his homie, Wet Em Up." Blue's bitch was so bad that Blake damn near wanted to shoot his shot at her. She smiled, showing her pretty, pearly white teeth and waved.

"Hi, I'm Kadijah, we got drinks in the kitchen and food in the oven, you guys can help yourselves to anything."

"I'm good on the food but I'll take something to drink and one of your friends to go with it," Wet Em Up said, causing everyone right there to laugh.

"I'm sure one of these hoes wouldn't mind giving you some attention," Kadijah replied just as a thick, dark-skinned beauty walked up. "Here go one of them right now," she giggled.

"What's so funny?" her friend asked.

"He was just asking about you," Kadijah lied, fronting Wet Em Up off.

"I know him," the friend said.

"Where you know me from?" Wet Em Up asked, letting his eyes roll over her thick body. Her big, round ass looked like it was ready to bust out of the onesie she had on.

"My friend Brittany fuck with your homie Nutso, and she brung me around a few times."

"Yo name Brandy or something right?" he asked as recognition started to kick in.

"No," she said quickly, cutting her eyes at him. "My name is Jamie." Blue nudged Blake and pulled him to the side so Wet Em Up could talk to Jamie in private. They went in the kitchen and poured shots of 1942 before taking a seat at the kitchen table.

"Man... bro, sometimes I be sitting back reminiscing and I find myself wishing I could go back in time and re-live all those younger days over when it was me, you, Shana, Lil Ced, Six and Millie. It ain't nothing I wouldn't trade for one of those epic apple wars." Blue chuckled before downing a shot and pouring himself another one.

"On folks nem grave, I be wishing the same shit," Blake agreed.

"Me and Shana started hating our father after he told us we couldn't be friends with y'all no more. At first, we didn't understand why, but even after I could understand, I still felt like that shit ain't have nothing to do with us kids. We just wanted to have fun." Blue paused to take a sip from his cup before continuing. "Y'all were my only real friends, The only friends I wanted," he said sadly.

Blake didn't respond. He couldn't, he was caught up in his thoughts. Images of Lil Ced, Six and Shana flashed through his mind. He took his cup to the head, hoping the burn from the liquor would temporarily took his mind off the past. Never in a million years did he think he would ever be kicking it with Blue again. Not after all the losses he took, not after him being the one who murdered a few members of Blue's family and kidnapped his baby sister. It was no way they should've been in the same room, but they were and strangely it felt good to be around him.

"Yeah, I hate that that shit went down how it did, all over a goofy ass nigga that was hatin on the niggas that was feedin him," was all he could muster up to say.

"Just imagine if my pops and Cordale never got into it," Blue paused to let him ponder a bit. "We would've been lit the fuck up!" he said with a huge smile. Both his father and Cordale were established in the streets on their own, so together you could only imagine they would've only been bigger. They both built their empires from selling nickel bags and even after they fell out, they both continued to run their bags up. "I really feel like we could still be lit together," he added, before knocking back another shot.

"You my boy and I wouldn't mind fucking with you, but them niggas from 47th had parts in killing my lil brother, so I would never be able to fuck with them on any level," Blake said, frowning up a bit.

"I understand that," Blue said, just as Millie entered the kitchen. At first glance, Blake didn't recognize her because she had gained a little weight. She was tall and thick, with a build similar to Megan Thee Stallion's. Her cinnamon-colored skin was flawless, and her hair was in knotless braids. Her big, round eyes grew large when they settled on Blake. "What's up Millie?" he asked, licking his lips.

"Hey, Blake." She waved. They held eye contact for a few awkward seconds before she turned to her brother, she started asking him questions about a salon. Blake wasn't too much paying attention to what they were discussing, he was too focused on staring at Millie. Her long juicy legs were covered in tattoos, as well as her arms. She was just as beautiful as Shana was, but she had more sex appeal to her if you asked him. She looked like a video vixen to him.

A few times Millie peeped over and caught Blake looking at her, but she said nothing about it. For Blake, it was kind of weird to be around her knowing what he did to her. He wanted to apologize but he knew in some cases, sorry wasn't enough.

The rest of the night went well. Blake got tipsy but didn't overdo it, knowing he had to be on point. To his surprise, nothing went down, nobody tried following him home, it wasn't an ambush waiting for him when he left out and he made it home safely.

Blue had cut into him about investing their money into something legit, a clothing line, a barbershop or some real estate. He was just throwing ideas out there, but he sounded like he was really tryna collaborate and turn their street earnings into generational wealth. Blake took that as a sign from God, because those were the same things Jala and Aisha were in his ear about, preparing for the future. He promised Blue they would get up together soon and chop it up on a legit, business level so they could come up with a solid plan.

Chapter 3

Chito entered the living room of his home, to see two grimy looking niggas sitting on his couch. One was a short, very dark-skinned skinny guy with sneaky, dark eyes and long dreadlocks. He was doing something on his phone that commanded his full attention. The other guy was brown-skinned and much taller with an athletic build, he also had long dreads and a few tats on his face, arms, neck and hands. The thing that stood out the most about him was the color of his eyes, they were blood red. Chito had met black people with hazel, gray and even ice blue eyes, but the man sitting on his couch was the only person he'd ever met with red eyes.

"Mo Money, what's up, primo?" Chito asked the darker of the two men, snatching his attention away from his phone.

Mo Money looked up and smiled at Chito. He always seemed to be smiling for some reason, he had a nice smile too, one that hid his fangs. Off first glance you wouldn't know how dangerous or cutthroat the man truly was. "What's up, King?" he asked, standing up to shake Chito's hand. He was short, about five-seven, and weighed about a hundred-fifty pounds soaking wet. He had low, dark eyes that seemed to watch everything. He could pass for a twenty-two-year-old, even though he was thirty years old.

"Glad to see you and Bang," Chito said, nodding towards the other guy. "How have you been?"

"I been all well, for a nigga of my caliber. Most of my opps dead and I'm still alive so I'm winning," Mo Money replied.

"You still out there moving like Bishop off *Juice*?" Chito asked and they shared a good laugh. The two had known each other for years. Mo Money's former plug was Chito's uncle Lopez and that was how they met. Chito was familiar with some of his dealings in the streets and how he was into it with his own homies, and he started calling him Tupac's character off the movie, *Juice*. That was their inside joke.

"You know that," Mo Money replied with a chuckle, even though he was dead ass serious. "So, what's this problem you need us to handle?" he asked, getting down to business.

"Are you familiar with the blocks 79th and Evans and 83rd and Vernon?"

"I know where that's at, that's Evans Mob and Get Wild Gang, what about them?"

"Blake, KD and Von…I need those three dead, I'm paying half a million apiece for their heads." Hearing the price tag on those guys' heads made Mo Money's smile broaden, showing his big, white teeth. Murder for hire had been his hustle for the past few years. He was once moving bricks of coke like they were going out of style, but after he was dragged into some bullshit behind one of his friend's fuck ups, his daughter was kidnapped and held for a two and a half-million-dollar ransom. He started robbing his clientele, as well as his family and friends, to scrape up the money to get his princess back.

That was a dark time in his life, a time where he lost himself and never really bounced back, mentally or emotionally. He lost all his credibility in the streets as a respectable hustler, and now everybody either feared him or they disliked him. Either way, they all kept their distance from him and showed him the utmost respect.

"Ooohhhh weeeeee! Why you ain't been called me and let me know what the fuck was going on?" he asked Chito with a mug. Chito could see the sparkle in his eyes and he knew that he was ready to leave and get on the hunt.

"Because, I thought we had it under control, to be honest—"

"But shorty nem been sliding back," Bang finished Chito's sentence, speaking for the first time.

"That's not what I was going to say but that about sums it up," Chito admitted honestly. This was his first time actually meeting Bang, he had heard plenty stories about him and the work he put in. He was a different type of dangerous than Mo Money was.

See, Mo Money was a man who knew how to chase a dollar. Bang, on the other hand, wasn't a money maker at all. All he'd ever known was slide, hunt and kill. He didn't care about money, he kept a lick lined up, so he never hustled. All he did was create chaos. He was like the Devil reincarnated. He was at war with his twin brother, who was almost as ruthless as he was. Bang was a cold-blooded killer and when he was in his mode not even women and children were safe.

"I been hearing about the pressure they been putting on y'all ass. The streets talk and right now they speaking highly of shorty nem, behind the way they been holding they own against y'all," Bang said with a small smirk on his face.

Mo Money caught the daggers Chito was shooting his homie, so he spoke up. "Say no more, primo, just make sure you have that money ready and don't be a dollar short, or I'ma do yo ass like Bishop did old man Quillis. 'He made a move!'" he quoted Tupac, making Chito erupt into a fit of laughter. The crazy part about it was that Chito knew that he was as serious as a heart attack.

"Another thing," Chito said, holding up a finger. "I got some of the best coke in the city and I know if can't nobody get it off, you can. So, what do you say we start doing business like good ol times?"

Mo Money frowned. The smile he was just wearing was now a scowl. That was never a good thing. "Come on now, Chito, you know I would never cross that line with you or any of yo peoples ever again. The last time could've ended badly," Mo Money paused and lowered his voice for the effect. "It should've ended badly, but I took my L and closed that chapter of my life. If I was ever to get some drugs from you, it would be from a robbery/homicide and not on consignment," he said.

Bang stood there with a wicked grin on his face like he was hoping that Chito took his homie's last comment personal, and some drama kicked off. He knew exactly what had his partner hot, but he kept his two cents to himself.

Chito stood there red-faced. Mo Money was lucky he needed him. A part of him wanted to put money on his head just for his big mouth. His rejection was one thing, but all that extra shit was uncalled for. Chito was more of a boss than Mo Money would ever be, so he really couldn't comprehend how he felt so comfortable speaking to him the way he was, especially in his home. Not only that, but Mo Money had the nerve to still be mean mugging him. "I meant you no disrespect, brother. I'm sorry you feel that way," he said humbly.

"It ain't shit, cuz," Mo Money said, extending his hand for a shake. They held eye contact, their gazes said way more than any words could say. "Have that bread ready for me," Mo Money added, before leading Bang out of the home.

Once in the driver's seat of his black Range Rover Evoque, Mo Money loosened up a bit. He was upset with himself for losing control and lashing out on Chito, but he had touched a nerve with what he said. The history between Chito's family and himself was deep. They had done things to him that turned his life upside down, things he would never forget.

"You wanna go back and smoke his ass?" Bang asked, noticing his friend's discomfort. He knew him well enough to know he was ready to kill.

"I do," Mo Money said with a crooked smile. "But then again, I don't."

"On Stone, you getting soft on me, ku," Bang teased, lighting up a half-smoked wood that was in the ashtray.

"Never," Mo Money replied with a straight face. "Matter of fact, since you sayin that dumb ass shit, I bet half a million that I kill Blake, KD and Von before you do."

Bang smacked his lips before taking a heavy drag off the wood. "You don't wanna make that bet. On Black Stone, you know how I get, law," he replied before taking another pull.

"On Stone, I bet I kill at least two out of the three," Mo Money shot back confidently.

"Bet, dummy." Bang chuckled, handing him the wood. This wasn't the first time the two had bet on something like that. They looked at the contracts they took on as nothing but challenges. They competed on who could do their victim the dirtiest, or who could kill the most when they had multiple targets. Catching bodies was like a sport to them and if it was, they considered themselves to be Stephen Curry and Klay Thompson when it came to shooting. They both had different outlooks on murder.

Bang killed because that's what he loved to do, he got a rush from taking lives, it made him feel better. Killing was his form of venting. The first thing he wanted to do when he got angry was to kill somebody. The first thing he wanted to do when he was hurting was to kill somebody. It was sad that he didn't have any other way to express himself.

Mo Money, on the other hand, killed because he felt like he had to. He didn't have too many friends left. He was at war with most of the guys he grew up with, he was even beefing with his younger cousin and former right-hand man Nutso, who was more like a brother to him. He loved his hood, but he didn't feel safe on his block or anywhere else, because of all the shit he'd done. He had hurt so many people that he claimed he loved, so now he had no trust for the loved ones that were still around.

He moved like an apex predator to make sure he was never prey. He had fucked up his reputation as the plug or even as a nigga you could do business with, so murder for hire was how he fed his family. He was accustomed to living a certain type of lifestyle, so he had to maintain a steady bankroll.

Mo Money rubbed the stubble on his chin with one hand and held the steering wheel with his other hand while navigating through the light traffic on the E-way. "Text Sheed and ask him where he at," he told Bang before turning up the Lil Durk song that they were listening to.

***

Blake woke up startled and reached for the Glock he kept on the nightstand beside his bed. His eyes darted around the room looking for danger but he found none. Aisha laid next to him naked, sleeping peacefully. She was snoring lightly, meaning she had to have been very tired. Blake climbed out of the bed still clutching his Glock and headed to the kitchen. He checked every room along the way just to be on the safe side. Once in the kitchen he went in the fridge and grabbed a carton of orange juice and lifted it to his lips.

Lately, paranoia had been getting the best of him. He couldn't hear a bump without thinking it was someone trying to get him. It'd been a few days since the last time he could get a full night's sleep. Tonight, was one of those nights where all he could do was toss, turn and stare at the ceiling. He decided to take a ride to clear his mind, plus he needed to smoke, and he was out of Backwoods. He crept back into his room and slipped on a pair of Nike sweats and a Nike t-shirt, he slid on a pair of Retro Jordan 3's and left out.

He drove aimlessly until stopping at a 7-Eleven on Dearborn and Van Buren to grab some Backwoods. He entered the store and headed straight for the back to grab himself a Fruit Water out of the fridge. On his way through one of the aisles, he passed a short, dark-skinned guy with long dreads. The guy's beady eyes locked onto Blake's chain. The guy looked grimy as hell, but he kept going without a word, he didn't even look back. Blake grabbed his drink and bought his woods at the register. When he left out the store, a dreadhead wearing a pair of shades was standing near the entrance.

"Aye, you got a light?" he asked Blake.

"Hell naw," Blake replied quickly just as the grimy-looking dreadhead was exiting the store. Blake thought he'd already left the store because he looked around for him before he left out and didn't see him. His intuition had told him to keep an eye on the guy.

"What about some weed?" the dreadhead asked Blake, still making his way closer to him.

"Naw, I don't got shit, bro," Blake gruffed with a little attitude. Out his peripheral, he saw the other dreadhead looming behind him. He knew a play when he saw one, so he knew he had to act before they did. He upped his Glock and fired wildly at the dreadhead with the glasses who was standing in front of him. He didn't try to line him up because he wasn't trying to kill the man, he simply wanted to make it to his car and get the fuck on.

The dreadhead jumped behind a mailbox and Blake bolted across the street to his car while firing wildly behind his back at the other dreadhead who had started shooting back. Blake made it to his car, glad he had left it running, he jumped in and sped off.

The shit that had just transpired had Blake hot. Hating ass, dirty ass niggas were always looking for a come up, then it was crazy how they were always ready to kill you when you weren't trying to give *your* shit up. Blake was truly becoming fed up with Chicago. He found a dark, quiet, nice looking side block to park on and roll up. He twisted two fat Backwoods before pulling off. He turned on "Hood Cycle" by G-Herbo and started driving aimlessly through the city. The exotic weed calmed him, but he was still overwhelmed with a bunch of feelings that he didn't know how to sort out.

It was always fucked up when you were feeling some type of way but didn't know why you were feeling how you were feeling or how to get that shit up outta you. That's why the streets were so fucked up. Everybody was angry or sad but nobody knew how to turn that pain, frustration and anger into positivity.

After an hour of riding Blake called Blue and asked him to meet him at the cemetery.

When Blue arrived, he was accompanied by Millie, who looked like she was on her way to star in a video shoot. She had on a Dior catsuit, a pair of Balenciaga runners and a thick, puffy Chanel coat. It was late, but she still had on a light coat of make-up.

"What's going on, bro?" Blue asked, taking a seat at one of the foldable chairs they kept at Shana and Lil Ced's gravesite. He could tell by the look of despondency on Blake's face that he had a lot on his mind. He had dark, heavy bags under his eyes, and he looked like he couldn't smile even if he wanted to, his whole aura was dismal. Blue also noticed the fifth of Rémy he had clutched in his grip.

"Tell me why I just got into a blick out coming out the seven-eleven on Van Buren," Blake replied before taking a swig from his bottle.

"With whom?" Blue asked, while breaking down a wood to roll up.

"Some niggas I didn't even fuckin know. I don't know if it was a hit or if it was a robbery gone bad."

"Could've been either one. It looks like that shit got you pressed."

"It do," Blake admitted and went on telling Blue all the things troubling him. He needed someone he could vent to that could speak back and he appreciated how both Blue and Millie listened while he poured his heart out. The liquor was starting to work its magic and the exotic they were smoking had him on cloud nine. "Ever since we had that talk at yo girl's crib, I been thinking about them apple wars like a mufucka," he said with a chuckle, causing Blue to laugh with him.

"Them bitches used to be bussin! Me, you and Millie, versus Shana, Lil Ced and Cragg. We used to be fucking them up!" Blue said excitedly. The pure joy in his voice made Millie, who had been sitting there silent the whole time, start giggling. "So, what was to Lil Ced?" Blue asked.

"What you mean what was to him?"

"He was my best friend growing up, but we was kids and after all that bullshit kicked off, we couldn't even kick it no more. I always wondered what kind of guy he had grown into."

"Aw…" Blake hit his bottle again and pondered his response. "Lil Ced was cool as hell. He was one of the realest niggas I ever met. He was spoiled as hell, but he was the type that made his pops buy me and Six some of the same clothes he had, so he wouldn't be the only one that was fresh. He would steal weed and give it to us to sell, so we could have some money. He was the type that didn't wanna shine on his own. He was funny as hell, he knew how to make some money and the nigga was loyal as hell," Blake said, staring at Lil Ced's headstone. "My boy was loyal to a fault," he said sadly. He was really trying his best to not get caught up in his feelings.

"I was hearing about him slidin and shit, they say my boy was puttin the belt on shit," Blue said, before flaming up a wood. The look on his face said he was excited hearing about Lil Ced.

Blake was a little hesitant to respond to that at first because Lil Ced had put in most, if not all of his work on Blue's people, so that was sort of a delicate topic. "Yeah, my boy was getting active," was all Blake said with a hint of a smile on his face. He and Lil Ced had done plenty of hits together. After his little brother lost his life behind his family's war, Lil Ced ultimately avenged his death by killing the man who killed him.

"Shana had told me everybody had turned on Lil Ced because of the love he had for her," Millie said, speaking for the first time.

"A lot of people started looking at him different when they found out what he was doing to protect y—" Blake caught himself and replaced y'all with "Shana."

"What about you?" Millie asked, staring at him intensely. Her brown eyes were searching for any signs of deception.

Blake lifted the bottle of Rémy to his lips and took a big gulp before answering. "At one point in time, I did start looking at him funny, and questioning his loyalty. I personally thought he was wrong for a lot of the shit he did. I used to tell him about himself all the time, but that was only because of all the loyalty shit he used to be screaming. In my mind I was like, how you so loyal and you out here fuckin with the opps?" Blake stopped speaking to take another swig. "But then, I realized his loyalty lied with Shana, not us. So, at the end of the day he was right all along, and we were wrong," he admitted.

The love Lil Ced had for Shana was so profound, so absolute and so taboo, it should've been a movie script or a romance novel. Their story was tragic, yet inspirational. Lil Ced's stories and ideologies alone was something that made Blake question the way he lived, and the decisions he made. Lil Ced inspired him to love better.

"That nigga saved my life," Blue said.

"Mines too," Millie said, shooting Blake a funny look that he caught. "He was a sweetheart and he held my sister down until the very end. I can't wait to find a man that's willing to love me the way he loved Shana," she added.

"I miss both of them," Blue said sadly. He was now in his feelings thinking about Shana. She was his closest sibling, and he took her death the hardest. "What ever happened to Ladale bitch ass?" he asked.

Blake explained Ladale's role in the grand scheme of things. He explained how Cordale found out he was the one who murdered Lil

Ced's mother and blamed it on Willis. He instigated the war for his own selfish reasons and it ultimately affected everyone but him. He had corrupted so many of Lil Ced's friends against him and had even gotten into Blake's head. He was the reason why Lil Ced couldn't come around and on top of all that, Ladale was a rat. He was all fucked up. When Blake was done filling Blue in on everything, Blue's face was twisted into a scowl.

"I always knew something was off about dude ass," he said.

"Yeah, but he not even a problem no more."

"He dead?"

"Might as well be," Blake said, hitting his bottle again. "Fuck that nigga doe," he said, getting up to stretch his long body. He was feeling groovy and was ready to move around. "What y'all bout to get into?" he asked.

"I'm bout to take my ass back in the crib. My bitch keep texting me and shit," Blue replied, getting up and dusting himself off. "It's good to be back locked in with you, big bro," he told, Blake giving him a half hug. "I'm here whenever you need me, bro," he promised, patting him on the back. Little did he know Blake needed to hear that, he was as lonely as he'd ever been and really felt like he had nobody.

"Fasho gang, hit my line tomorrow," Blake said, heading for his car.

***

After leaving the cemetery, Blake decided to ride through one of the Latin Kings' hoods on the east side, it was a little after 1:00 am. He knew the chances of someone being outside was slim to none, but he was optimistic, so he still rode through. On 97th Street, right off of Commercial, he saw a yellow and black Hummer H3 sitting at a red light. The truck had tints, but the gold and black paint job was enough for him to assume the driver was one of the Kings. He rolled down his window and pulled right next to the Hummer. He started unloading his clip in the truck, the driver tried to pull off and swerve around a Hyundai but crashed into a minivan.

Blake pulled his car next to the smashed-up Hummer and emptied the rest of his clip into the window before screeching off. That wasn't enough for Blake, he needed to shoot somebody all in their face to satisfy his thirst for blood. He was on his way through the BarNone's block before he received a *FaceTime* call from Jala.

"Hey bae," she said, smiling into the camera, showing her deep dimples. Blake could see she was at home sitting in the tub.

"What's up?" he replied dryly.

"Ugh! What's wrong with you?" she asked, frowning her beautiful face up.

"I got a lot on my mind," Blake replied, peeking at his rearview.

"A lot like what? Cause you been actin real funny lately. You must've found yourself a new bitch."

"The shit that's going on with Lil Moe and KD got me stressing the fuck out. We got too many opps to be beefing with each other. I was fake beefing with Lil Ced before he killed himself and we left off on a bad note. I don't want it to be the same way with bro nem," he vented, ignoring her comment about him having a new bitch.

"If you don't want it to be like that, then make it right with them," Jala said, completely blind to the real reason why him and KD were beefing. He had given her a fake story about them being into it over some money. "You need to do something, because I'm tired of the way you been acting towards me."

"How I been acting?" Blake asked, watching a black Dodge Durango that had been behind him for about two blocks now. It wasn't much he could do because he had already emptied his clip. He sent a text to Wet Em Up, who was still in the 106th trap and told him to be on point, because he was being followed and was about to lead them to him.

"You been distant as hell, we barely talk, and I see you maybe once a week. I'm starting to feel like a side bitch," Jala admitted.

"Stop that, you know I love yo lil pie face ass to death," Blake replied honestly. He kept talking to Jala while making his way to the Hundreds. As he suspected, the Durango was following him. He tried to not run any lights or stop signs, because he didn't want his pursuers to know he was on to them. Once he got on 103rd and

Indiana, he sent a text to Wet Em Up and told him to shoot the Black Durango up.

Blake could see two men dressed in black standing on each side of the street as he rode past the 106th trap. The sound of two Micro Dracos going off sounded like a scene out of a *Transformers* movie. Jala heard the shots going off and flinched, even though she was in the safety of her own home.

"Are they shooting at you?" she asked Blake, who chuckled at the expression on her face.

"Naw, I'm good, baby. Finish telling me about your day," he said, speeding away from the scene.

The next day, Blake woke up early and as he was scrolling through his *Facebook* timeline, he saw his homie Tune had gotten killed. He *FaceTimed* Lil Trav to find out how Tune had gotten killed and found out, Tune was in the car with Lil Moe, and they had gotten blown down in the Hundreds. Halfway through the story, he realized it was Lil Moe and Tune who were following him last night. Nine times out of ten they were trying to kill him, so he didn't feel bad that Tune had gotten his dumb ass killed trying to be sneaky. He didn't fill Lil Trav in on what he knew, he didn't want to front his hand and he wasn't sure whose side Lil Trav was actually on. Being unable to trust the ones that he called his friends was really starting to fuck with him.

The crazy thing was, the further away he kept his friends, the closer he was becoming to Wet Em Up and Blue. He kicked it with Wet Em Up on the daily and was giving him his own pounds to jug, on top of the money he was making off working the trap with Boothie.

Blake was also spending more and more time with Blue. It was a different vibe when they were together. They would go to all type of events that Blake and KD would've never gone to together, like yacht parties, fashion shows and business conventions. Blue was connected to a lot of people and seemed as though he was really trying to transition into a businessman.

The type of women he fucked with were nurses, dentists and entrepreneurs, who wouldn't look twice at the average hood nigga.

Blake admired how one minute Blue could be dressed in the latest designer and the next minute, he would be wearing a turtleneck, some slacks and a pair of designer loafers. He was versatile and knew how and when to switch it up. He never presented himself as a thug. The only downside with hanging with Blue was Millie, he always felt uncomfortable when they were in the same room. She never said or did anything to make him feel that way, it was most likely because of their history. Whatever it was, he always felt weird around her.

One day Von had called Blake to let him know KD had asked him about his dealings with him. He said KD asked about the weed Blake was putting on D Block and he had even asked for him to set Blake up for him. Von D fucked with both of them hard and them being into it put him in a fucked-up position, because he didn't want to choose sides and he wasn't playing the middle. He wanted no part in the beef they had going on. He had good things going on with both of them and refused to ride with either one against the other.

The only reason he called Blake was to put him on his toes, he would've did the same for KD if Blake had called on some bullshit. He had told KD that any idea of catching Blake on D Block and doing something to him was dead. Blake was starting to feel like KD was forcing his hand to kill him and something he really didn't want to do. But he couldn't sit back and get killed. He had a lot of thinking to do.

Molotti

Chapter 4

Cordale entered the federal courtroom wearing a Louis Vuitton suit that was tailored to fit him perfectly. His lawyer, Jerry Bischoff, stood at his table wearing a confident smirk. This was their third day of trial and none of the government's witnesses were showing up. The prosecutor on the case tried to paint the picture that Cordale was something like a gang chief, and was responsible for the missing witnesses, but he didn't have any credible evidence to support his theory.

All in all, Jerry Bischoff was eating the government up, making their case look weaker and weaker.

"How're you feeling today?" he asked Cordale, who took a seat next to him.

"I'm straight, hopin we can get this shit over with today," Cordale replied, before scratching the long scar going across his neck. Months ago, he was the victim of a brutal stabbing by the Latin Kings. They stabbed and sliced him over twenty times, and almost succeeded in killing him. He had scars all over his face, chest and neck from the attack, so every time he looked in the mirror, he was reminded of the attempt on his life.

"Well, if none of the government's witnesses appear today, then the judge will push for closing arguments," Jerry was explaining just as the bailiff asked everyone to rise for the judge. The Honorable Judge Thomas Kunkel was a fat, white man with thin silver hair and low eyes that appeared to be closed. He entered the courtroom and took a seat. "Mr. Karlowski, is the government ready to put any witness on the stand?" he asked the prosecutor. "Yes, Your Honor," the prosecutor, Michael Karlowski, replied nervously. His skinny body shifted from side to side.

"Ok then," Judge Kunkel grunted, looking over some paperwork sitting neatly on his desk.

Cordale shot Jerry a look that showed his own nervousness he felt on the inside. He knew for sure he had gotten all of the witnesses out of the way, so to hear the government had a witness who was ready to get on the stand and testify, had him shaken up a bit.

Moments later, a raggedy looking, brown-skinned guy with crooked, yellow stained teeth, and a nappy fro, came out of the back and took a seat at the stand. His eyes darted around the courtroom. When he locked eyes with Cordale, he quickly averted his gaze down to his hands, which were folded on his lap. The guy looked vaguely familiar to Cordale, but he couldn't quite place where he knew him from. He looked like a fucking hype.

Michael Karlowski stepped up and cleared his throat. "Hello sir, can you please state your name for the courtroom?"

"Bumpy," the guy said raspily.

"Your real name," Michael said sharply.

"Aw, my bad. Darnell Collins," Bumpy said with a smile.

"And do you know who Mr. Cordale Marshall is?"

"Yeah, I—"

"Can you please point him out?" Michael asked and Bumpy pointed a finger at Cordale. "And how do you know Cordale?"

"Through his brother, Ladale. We used to hustle together," Bumpy said and Cordale sighed. The last thing he needed was for one of Ladale's weird, broke ass friends to testify on him and get him slayed by the jury. Luckily for him, he'd never done a damn thing with Bumpy, he didn't even know him.

"Who used to hustle together? You and Cordale, or you and Ladale?" Michael asked.

"Me and Ladale," Bumpy answered, still looking down at his hands.

"Have you ever sold drugs with, or for Cordale?"

"He was the plug."

"So, you're saying Cordale supplied you with drugs?"

"No, not me directly, but to my knowledge that's where everybody got their pounds from."

Cordale was shocked by Bumpy's testimony. Not only did he not remember who this bum was, but he was positive he had never supplied him with anything. He leaned over and whispered in Jerry's ear, "I never did any type of business with that bum."

"Don't worry," Jerry replied.

Michael Karlowski questioned Bumpy for a whole thirty minutes before Jerry stood up to cross examine him. "So, Mr. Collins, have you ever personally received any drugs from Cordale?" Jerry asked.

"Uh-um, not from him, but that's where his brother got his shit from and I was getting it from him," Bumpy said, stumbling over his words.

"So, you've never witnessed Cordale handling any drugs with your own two eyes?"

Bumpy shot Jerry a dirty look before mumbling, "No."

"So, how could you say he was the 'plug'?"

"Because that was the word on the street, and it was obvious. He wore the best clothes, wore diamond chains and watches, lived in a nice home and drove luxury cars. It wasn't a secret he was getting money," Bumpy explained. He looked over at Cordale and the look he was shooting him let him know he was living on borrowed time. He knew he had no business testifying on him, but the feds were offering to drop the Armed Habitual Criminal case he was fighting in the state, so he jumped on the opportunity and sold his soul. The barrage of questions Jerry fired at Bumpy discredited his whole testimony. He couldn't testify that he'd ever been in the same room as Cordale.

At first, Cordale was nervous but now he sat there with a confident smirk on his face. Jerry had assured him that today would be the last day he spent in jail. He was so confident in it, he told him he would give him a hundred thousand back if he didn't win in trial.

It took the jury less than three hours to deliberate and come back with a verdict. Despite the mask of confidence he wore, Cordale was as anxious as he'd ever been. Butterflies fluttered around his stomach and his heart was pounding out of his chest. A guilty verdict would sit him down for a mandatory minimum of ten years, he wasn't prepared to spend all that time in jail. He knew he would be financially straight but mentally, jail would wear him out. One word would determine his future. He would either be going home later that day or spending a long time in the federal prison system.

He uttered a silent prayer asking God to watch over him and bless him with an innocent verdict.

On the other side of the courtroom, Michael Karlowski sat at the table looking a hot mess. This was the biggest case of his career and in the beginning, it looked like an open and closed case. He had all his ducks in a row to convict Cordale and now everything had fallen apart. Witness after witness had either come up dead or was now unable to be found. The one witness he did have, he knew wasn't credible, but he put him on the stand anyway, hoping at least one member of the jury would believe him and they'd end up with a hung jury. It was a Hail Mary, but he was desperate, so he had to throw it.

To Cordale it felt like an eternity before the judge finally mumbled the word, "Innocent." Cordale's lips spread into a wide smile and he felt as it the weight of the world had been lifted from his shoulders. He suppressed his desire to shed a few tears of joy. He looked back in the audience to see Blake sitting next to Aisha, they were both smiling at him. Von D sat next to them and KD, along with a few of the older folks were sitting on the other side of the courtroom. Everyone wore smiles. Cordale shook Jerry's hand and gave him a half hug before exiting the courtroom.

It took a few hours for the feds to process Cordale out of their system. He exited the MCC and inhaled a lungful of fresh air. It was chilly out and he wore his gray jogging suit and a pair of orange Karate shoes. He saw a black Audi R8 with tinted windows sitting there and headed for it. The locks popped and he slid in the backseat.

"Hey, Daddy, welcome home!" Aisha beamed, turning around in her seat to give Cordale a hug.

"Hey, princess," he said after giving her a kiss on the forehead. "What's up, G?" he asked Blake playfully jabbing him in the ribs. He was ecstatic to be free.

"What's up, old man? I told you I was gone get you up outta that jam," Blake replied, looking at him through the rearview mirror.

"Yeah, you did, and I appreciate everything you've done for me."

"Man, stop that soft ass shit," Blake said, cutting him off. He was like a father to him so he owed him no thanks. Blake couldn't even imagine how fucked up his life might've been if Cordale and Lil Ced hadn't welcomed him into their family. He more than likely would've been somewhere broke, starving and gangbanging.

The ride to Blake's home was a mostly quiet one. Cordale gazed out of his window, just appreciating the fact that he was now a free man. The simplest things were now so beautiful to him. Jail had its way of changing a man's perspective. Small things like bodywash, being able to eat a hot meal whenever you wanted to, a woman's soft touch, and being able to shit and shower privately were appreciated more after a man did time. Having your own soft bed, your own clothes and cable were valued more. Life was more precious after you've been in a position where you were alive but not living. He missed everything about being free and he was silently taking it all in.

Once at Blake's house, Cordale showered and got dressed in a Givenchy outfit Aisha picked out for him. "Take me to Ladale," he told Blake after he was done getting dressed.

Blake laughed, he laughed so hard that his stomach started cramping up. He grabbed his stomach and doubled over in laughter. "Slow down, Unc, you just got out," he said, wiping tears from his eyes. He knew Cordale was dead ass serious and that's what made it so funny. "We got a good night planned out for you. You gone eat good, get you some good pussy and get you some good sleep, and tomorrow we can go see dude goofy ass."

"A'ight man," Cordale said reluctantly.

The first thing they did was go to Ruth Chris' Steakhouse to have a welcome home dinner. Blake invited everybody who he thought he could trust to the dinner. Aisha had an attitude because he invited Jala, but she had enough respect not to ruin her father's celebration. Aisha, Blake, Von D, Jala and Cordale all sat at the same table.

"Man, I thought them bitches had killed me," Cordale said, rubbing the scar on his neck after telling them the story about how the Latin Kings had pushed up on him.

"On Stone, we made them boys stop coming outside after that shit. Every night we were slidin through they shit," Von D boasted. The whole dinner, he had been boasting and bragging, trying to impress Cordale. They didn't know each other too well but just like he did Blake, Cordale took Von D in and changed his life for the better.

Von D had heard a million stories about Cordale and he knew now that he was home, the money train was about to take off, and Cordale was the conductor.

When Blue and Millie entered the restaurant, Cordale's eyes lit up. He hadn't seen them since Lil Ced and Shana's funeral and even then, he didn't pay them too much mind. He couldn't while he was saying his last goodbyes to his only child, and then the feds snatched him right up. Blue almost looked the same as he did when he was a shorty, but he was taller, slimmer, with a light mustache. His ice blue eyes were still bright with joy. Millie looked just like her mother did back in the day, she just had way more body. Cordale looked at her ass and wondered if she had gotten any work done.

"What's up, Unc? Long time no see," Blue said, bopping towards Cordale, who got up and embraced him with a half hug.

"Lil Blue," Cordale said with a smile. "You ain't so little no more. And look at you," he said turning to Millie and giving her a tight hug. "You looking just like your mother."

Blue and Millie took a seat at the table and ordered their food. The dinner went smoothly even though it was one of the most awkward situations that Blake had ever been in. He had Jala sitting next to him while Aisha glowered at them from across the table. Every now and then, she would send him a text or "accidently" kick his foot, if she felt like he was doing too much with Jala in her face.

On the other hand, Blake kept catching Millie watching him, her gaze was alluring yet cautionary. It was hard for Blake to read, but being the street nigga he was, he put his safety first and had Wet Em Up and Boothie waiting in the parking lot looking for anything suspicious, not just from them but just in case the guys pulled a stunt.

Halfway through the dinner, KD and Lil Moe waltzed into the restaurant smelling like a pound of exotic. Blake didn't see them at first, he only saw the expression on Aisha's face go from smug to tense, that's what made him look back to see the two approaching their table. KD's eyes were bloodshot red and his hand dipped to his waistline when he saw Blake and Blue chopping it up like they were the best of friends.

"What type of opp shit y'all got going on in here?" he asked bemused. Seeing how cordial the two were together had his blood boiling. Blue's big brother was the one who shot KD up a few years ago. KD was so mad he wanted to kill both Blue and Blake right then and there.

"They're cool, they with me," Cordale said calmly. He matched KD's icy glare with a firm stare of his own. His look told KD it was best if he just stood down and left it alone. "What's up, Jala?" he asked flirtatiously, he was intentionally trying to get under Blake's skin now.

"Hey," Jala replied dryly. She knew it was animosity between him and her man, and she was riding with hers until the wheels fell off.

"Why haven't you texted me today? Let me find out you actin funny," he replied, catching the hint of attitude in Jala's tone.

"Don't do that," she snapped. "We not even gone play like that," she added, causing Aisha to chuckle.

Blake sat there biting the inside of his jaw, trying to control his anger that was tempting to erupt. KD was mad and in his feelings about Blake taking his bitch, and now he was playing with Jala. Blake didn't like that one bit.

The tension at the table was so thick, everyone noticed it, but no one was comfortable enough to speak on it. Cordale tried to keep things cool by making small talk but KD constantly made snide remarks about Blake or Aisha. His jealousy and envy showed through his blatant disrespect. He wore his feelings on his sleeve and wasn't ashamed of his pain.

Lil Moe, who was sky high off X pills, mean mugged Blake the whole time, until Blake gave him the attention he was looking for.

"Fuck is you looking at?" Blake asked angrily.

"On Stone, you right here sitting with the mufuckas that killed yo lil brother, you ain't on shit, miss me with that tough shit," Lil Moe spat with venom in his words. He thought his comment would hurt Blake, but it didn't. He could say whatever he wanted to say, but everyone at the table knew he had got the get back for his brother's murder.

"You just make sure you don't be the next mufucka that get killed," Blake replied cooly.

"Y'all shut the fuck up and leave that shit alone!" Cordale boomed, causing a few people around the restaurant to stare at their table, trying to figure out what was going on. Everyone sat there in an awkward silence for a few minutes until KD smacked his lips.

"So, you cool with all the snake ass shit this nigga got going on?" he asked with his face twisted up.

"This not the time nor the place for us to be discussing that shit, so talk about something else or shut the fuck up," Cordale said with authority.

"You right," KD said, getting up from his seat and storming out of the restaurant. Lil Moe was right behind him. Blake immediately shot a text to Wet Em Up and told him to watch the two and make sure they left the parking lot.

Cordale looked around the table to see that all eyes except for Blake's were on him. At that moment it hit him that he was finally back home, finally back in charge and it was a list of things he needed to repair. "Don't worry about him," he told Blue. "I'll talk to him and let him know he gotta put his feelings in his back pocket," he added, before taking a sip from his glass of wine.

"Fuck that nigga," Blake grumbled.

"Blake, get the fuck on. I'll talk to you tomorrow," Cordale said, dismissing him from the dinner. He demanded respect and it seemed like everybody seemed to have forgotten who was in charge. Blake got up, dropped a gang sign with Blue and said his goodbyes to Millie before leading Jala out of the restaurant.

"I run this shit!" Cordale said to himself, more than anyone else at the table. He had never witnessed his shorties act in the manner they had just acted in. He hadn't been out for a day yet and he was already seeing why his operation fell apart. Blake and KD were controlled by their emotions, they didn't think logically, they didn't act with reason, they acted in conjunction with their feelings. That was the main reason why nothing was the same. Cordale smiled because he was back and he knew for certain he would coach his team back into the finals.

The next morning, Cordale woke up in his California king sized bed and said a silent prayer, thanking God for his freedom. Next to him a pretty, chocolate woman slept peacefully. He lifted the covers to see her perfect naked body and thought about waking her up to some good dick, but he had more important things on his mind. He rolled out of bed, went to handle his hygiene and got dressed before *FaceTiming* Blake.

"What's up?" Blake answered, rubbing the crust out of the corner of his eyes. Cordale could see Aisha snuggled next to him sleeping.

"Let's go handle that business," he said.

"Aight, let me get the money together first and then I'ma call P Ball and let him know we ready."

"How long that's gone take?"

"A couple hours."

Cordale was bothered but he didn't show it. "Aight," he said before hanging up in Blake's face. Since he had a few hours to kill, he grabbed the Glock 19 Blake had given him and left out.

Half an hour later, he was at Burr Oaks cemetery, standing in front of TayTay's headstone. It had been a long time since he had been able to visit his lover's resting place. He missed her dearly. He thought about how in a few hours he would be face-to-face with Ladale, his older brother, the man who murdered her. He had a million questions that he was prepared to ask him. He needed to know what drove him to take his woman from him.

Cordale's life had been nothing but a downward spiral since losing her, and the only thing that could give his soul some closure was a conversation with Ladale. Cordale sat a dozen yellow roses in front of TayTay's headstone. Yellow was her favorite color. He pulled out a cigarette and lit it up. The cold winter air somehow crept through his Moncler coat and sent chills down his body.

Something told him to look back and he peeped over his shoulder to see a hooded figure headed his way. The guy had on a red Canada Goose coat, and his long dreads hung out the hood. Cordale's hand dropped to his waistline where his Glock rested but recognition kicked in and he relaxed, sort of. "If it ain't the big bad wolf himself," he joked.

Mo Money smiled, showing his big white teeth. His smile was what made you assume that he was just a venom-less snake. His smile was warm, friendly and inviting but that was all an illusion. His venom was deadly and not many, if any, could say they survived an encounter with his fangs. "Welcome home, old school," he rasped, giving Cordale a half-hug. "How long you been out?"

"Shit, not even a whole twenty-four hours," Cordale replied, trying to read his body language. Mo Money and bullshit ran hand in hand, if one was around, then the other was always close by. "What's been up with you?"

Mo Money took a deep breath like he had a lot on his mind. His dark eyes darted around the cemetery searching for any signs of danger. "I been all well, still up to the same shit," he said, flashing a sinister grin.

"So, what do I owe for this visit?" Cordale asked sarcastically. His hand was inching towards his Glock. He knew it was no coincidence he was at the cemetery.

"You cool, man," Mo Money assured him, picking up on his vibe. "My lil homie Von D... you know him, right?" Mo Money asked, already knowing the answer.

"Yeah, that's my lil cousin."

"That's my fucking boy," Mo Money said with a smile, and this time the smile was genuine. "The Kings want him dead behind some shit he did with yo shorties, they got a lot of money on they head and they really getting desperate."

"And let me guess, they came to you to get the job done?" Cordale asked, cutting him off.

Mo Money nodded and scanned the cemetery. "I would never hurt my boy or let anything happen to him, I got too much love for him."

"Thanks."

"But the same doesn't go for Blake or KD," Mo Money told Cordale. "That's easy money and I gotta eat too."

"How much would it take to convince you to fall back of them too?" Cordale asked, ready to break the bank for his family. He was sure Blake and KD could take care of themselves, but Mo Money was a different animal. If the price was right, he wouldn't relent until he got one, if not both of them.

"You know it don't work like that."

"So, what the fuck you here for?" Cordale snapped.

"Somebody in y'all circle working with the Kings, feeding them information and giving them locations and shit. I don't know who it is, but I know for a fact somebody playing both sides."

"How do you know doe?"

"Me and Chito got a rapport that goes back years, we talk a little and that's how I got locations and shit. Whoever it is he's spoon-feeding Chito the information. He using y'all as his trump card to stay alive. Like I said, Blake and KD... I gotta check they ass in and collect that million-dollar ticket. But Von D, he family, so relay this message for me," Mo Money said, throwing his hood back over his head. "Take my number," he told Cordale, who pulled out his phone and saved his number.

Mo Money walked off, leaving Cordale with something to think about. It was a snake in their circle, a snake that was willing to trade their lives for his, instead of standing ten toes with his niggas. Cordale pulled out another Newport and flamed it up. He hated the younger generation, they had no loyalty, no principles and no morals. It was every man for himself. The shorties were so cutthroat that loyalty and honor was shunned. Nowadays, you were considered a lame if you weren't down for the double cross. That shit made Cordale sick to his stomach. He left the cemetery to go meet up with Von D and let him know they had a snake in their grass.

***

Blake sat on his bed putting rubber bands on ten thousand-dollar stacks of money. Aisha sat Indian style next to him, helping him count out and band the money. She still had a slight attitude for all of the love and affection he'd shown to Jala at her father's dinner. She felt a little better now because he came home to her and fucked her good, before rolling over and falling asleep.

"My daddy crazy for paying all of this money just to talk to a nigga," she said, not looking up from the task at hand. "He could've just had them kill him and saved three hundred thousand."

"You right, but it's way deeper than you know. Ladale killed Lil Ced's mother and started a war that cost us more than you could imagine. Yo pops want answers. Why this and why that, I would want the same thing."

"Why do you think he did all that stuff?"

"I don't know," Blake replied with a shrug. "Yo uncle weird as hell, that nigga a hater and a master manipulator. I feel like he had been hating on yo pops and Willis from day-one. Plus, he was jealous of their relationship and that's why he did so much to tear them apart," Blake said. He didn't really care why Ladale made the decisions that he made, all he cared about was Cordale giving the green light to kill his soft ass. He really wanted to be the one who did it, because to him that would be his way of avenging Lil Ced, Shana and Six.

"So, my uncle was a rat *and* a snake huh?" Aisha asked with a giggle.

"Basically," Blake replied dryly.

After a few minutes of dry silence, Aisha finally spoke what was on her mind. "I don't like how disrespectful you were at my father s dinner," she said.

"What the fuck is you talkin about?" Blake asked, screwing up his face.

"The way you was all up Jala's ass, right in my face."

"That's my bitch!"

"And what am I?" she asked.

Blake silently thumbed through blue-faced, hundred-dollar bills, while thinking of a worthy response. "I love you," he finally said.

Aisha smacked her lips and twisted her face up. "I didn't ask you if you loved me or not. I asked what am I to you?" she replied angrily.

"You mean a lot to me. Like I said, I—" Blake was saying until Aisha jumped out of the bed and stormed out of the room. He wasn't in the mood for her bitching about a relationship that he was in, way before she came into the picture. He was sure she was in the hallway or bathroom, waiting on him to come running after her, but she had him fucked up if that's what she thought. After counting out two hundred thousand dollars, Blake *FaceTimed* P Ball.

"What's up, gang?" P Ball answered "Big bro home and he ready for that package you been holding for him. We got the rest of that lil pay-pay for you too," Blake said, flipping the camera to the stacks of money he had all over his bed.

P Ball flashed his signature smile at the sight of the money. "Aight, I'm ready whenever y'all ready."

"I'm bout to go pick up the big homie and Von D, and we'll be right to you."

"Bet," P Ball said and hung up. He didn't show it, but he was pissed that Blake was bringing Von D. He knew about the bag on Blake's head, and he wanted to cash his ass in. He couldn't do it with Von D there, he had too much love and respect for Von to blatantly disrespect him by smoking his mans, P Ball's right-hand man.

Vic was never around when he met up with Blake because Vic couldn't trust himself not to shoot off his face. They had lost a few friends while beefing with Blake nem and the scars were still fresh. P Ball was glad everything had played out the way it did because they checked a bag fucking with Blake nem. Two-hundred-thousand-dollar drug deals, plus the four hundred thousand dollars they got for snatching up Ladale, P Ball and his boys were *sitchy*, they were all eating good.

It took almost an hour before Blake, Von D and Cordale were pulling up on 114th and State P Ball was sitting in his car with C Dot, they both jumped out and met Von nem in front of the trap. Blake handed P Ball a Bape backpack holding the two hundred thousand dollars.

Cordale had butterflies in his stomach, he had been anticipating this moment ever since Detective Pendarves helped him discover that Ladale was the one who murdered TayTay. While sitting in jail, he would often lay back and fantasize about the day he would be able to talk to Ladale face-to-face. He had the whole conversation mapped out in his head, he only needed Ladale to fill in the blanks.

As he followed Blake and P Ball through the abandoned home, he started to forget every question he planned on asking, he was getting more and more anxious with every step he took. The basement of the home was musty and dark. P Ball found the light switch the wall and flicked it on. When Ladale's eyes adjusted to the light, the first person he saw was Blake. "Fuck you doing here, bitch ass nigga?" he asked. His breath was so bad, Blake could smell it from halfway across the room.

Instead of responding, Blake flashed Ladale a sinister grin and stepped aside. Cordale stood there with an inscrutable expression on his face. The sight of his brother standing there sent chills through Ladale's body. He just knew the feds would make sure he stayed in jail for a long time. When he started cooperating, the lead agent on the case ensured him they had a very strong case against Cordale, and to see him standing there, staring at him with a deadly gaze had Ladale ready to kill himself.

"Y'all good?" P Ball asked, feeling the tension in the room rise to a different level.

"Hell yeah," Cordale spoke up. "Everybody can leave, I got this," he said.

"I'ma stay with you," Von D offered.

"Naw, I'll call you when I'm ready to be picked up," Cordale said. Everybody knew what this moment meant to him, so nobody argued with him. In seconds, he was alone in the trap, just him and his brother.

"Bruh, what the fuck was you thinking, having yo peoples kidnap me and holding me like this!" Ladale snapped. "I knew that nigga Willis finessed you into turn—"

"Shut the fuck up!" Cordale roared. His deep baritone echoed through the basement.

"Bruh, I'm not blind to your bullshit anymore. I'm a grown ass man and I can't be manipulated by you, so cut that bullshit out. I seen yo 5K1 with my own eyes, you was the government's star witness."

"Bruh, do you think I would've actually got on that stand and testified on you? Come on now, be serious," Ladale said and Cordale hit him with a stale face. He kept speaking. "They was talking about Willis was gone testify that I murdered his brother if they dropped him off the case, so I got down on his ass first. I was gone put everything on him to save both of us."

The fear in Ladale's eyes excited Cordale. It was like he was feeding off the fear that radiated from him. "You think this about you being a rat?" he asked, grabbing two crates, stacking them up and taking a seat on top of them, directly in front of Ladale.

"Yeah," Ladale replied with a nod.

"This shit way deeper than that." Ladale looked at the ground for a few seconds while trying to think about what he could be so mad about. Deep down, he knew his brother had about a million reasons to hate him, so trying to pinpoint one was hard. "You doing all this over the loads I hijacked? Come on bruh, that shit was slight, you wasn't hurt by that little shit."

Cordale chuckled. Deep down, he always suspected he was the one who was hijacking his trucks that delivered his weed. The love he had for him had him blind and in denial, he didn't want to believe his big brother was getting down on him, not when he was feeding him and making sure he never went broke. When Lil Ced was going through his situation and he hijacked one of the delivery trucks, Ladale tried to convince Cordale he was the one doing it since he was up to age, but the hijackings had been going on way before Lil Ced was able to do it.

For a second, Cordale actually believed it and was disappointed in his son. Now to hear it come out the horse's mouth, he was infuriated.

"This ain't about no drugs either," Cordale said flatly.

Ladale smacked his crusty lips and frowned. "I know you ain't trippin like this over me missing Lil Ced's funeral. I was scared you was gone let Willis get down on me, so I chose not to come. You really can't blame me for that, bruh."

Cordale stared daggers at him for what seemed like an eternity before he cleared his throat and asked. "Why did you kill TayTay?" The question made Ladale's face drop and he couldn't hold his brother's gaze, so he dropped his head. Cordale watched him stare at the floor for five full minutes before speaking again. "Bruh, if you ever had any type of love for me you would tell me why you did what the fuck you did! Give me some closure to the situation, because when you took her from me, you took my life. You subjected me to a lifetime of misery when you decided to take that woman out of my life. You fucked up my son's life and I at least deserve to know why you took her," Cordale said, feeling a lump form in his throat.

Ladale slowly shook his head from left to right. When he looked up and locked eyes with his brother, it was almost as if he could see the dark cloud hovering over him. He was certain he had gotten away scot-free with TayTay's murder; no one ever questioned him. No one ever suspected for it had been him. Everybody was so sure it was Willis behind the murder, they overlooked him. Now he was stuck thinking if Cordale really knew it was him or was he just fishing.

"Bruh, what the fuck are you talkin—"

"Don't fuckin play with me right now!" Cordale yelled, spit flying from his mouth with every word. "The lead detective showed me a video of your car pulling up to the crib. You was there for a while and then you left. TayTay's time of death was somewhere around the time when you were there. I know it was you, bruh, I just wanna know why," Cordale said in a much calmer tone. His voice was breaking, and he was holding back tears.

"Just kill me, bruh," Ladale replied, shaking his head.

"That's the point, I don't want to kill you, bruh. If I wanted you dead, you could've been dead. I just want some closure and then we can go our separate ways." Ladale shook his head again. He knew that what he said next would crush Cordale more than anything. He thought about lying, but he spent his whole life lying and running away from the truth. For all the good his little brother did for him in his lifetime, he repaid him with wrong after wrong. If telling the truth was his chance to right some of those wrongs, then he would give Cordale the closure he so desperately wanted. Ladale took a deep breath before starting. . .

Molotti

Chapter 5
Summer 1996

Ladale was riding in his two-door Chevy with his boy O Dog. they were fresh off a lick and looking for another victim. Ladale lit up a Newport and turned down the volume to the Biggie Smalls song that was playing on the radio. "What you bout to do folks, cause it look like we ain't bout to find another lick right now," he said to O Dog.

"Shit you can drop me off on the block."

Ladale pulled up on 47th Place to see Cordale and Willis standing on Willis' porch. A brand-new Chevy Nova was sitting in front of Willis' house. Ladale parked, he and O Dog hopped out and approached Willis' porch. "Who shit is that?" Ladale asked, nodding at the old-school after shaking up with Cordale and Willis.

"That's my shit," Willis said with a prideful smile. He and Cordale were sellin weed together and they both were making progress in the game. The car was Willis' first big purchase.

"I'm about to go buy me a black one," Cordale said, standing next to Willis. They were best friends and stayed getting matching items. When he bought himself a sixteen-inch gold Cuban link chain, Willis did too. When they went to prom with their senior girlfriends, they wore the same royal blue suit. They were like two peas in a pod.

"Damn, when y'all gone cut me in so I can be a part of the mix?" Ladale asked, staring at the Chevy.

Cordale and Willis were selling weed. At first, they started off selling for one of their big homie's named Boogie, but after stacking so much they were able to put their money together and grab a pound and now they were hustling for themselves. They were now grabbing three pounds. They would each get one and then split the third one. They knew how to stack their money and make it look good. They dressed in the hottest fashions they'd bought from some booster bitches they were fucking on. They drove nice cars and they hosted the best parties, that was another way they made money. The parties they hosted were legendary, the whole hood looked forward to them.

Ladale had been on their asses about them putting him in play, but he proved to be a fuck-up and neither one of them were willing to risk fucking up what they had going on for Ladale. Being the manipulator he was, he convinced Cordale to think about putting him on. Cordale knew deep down he was too lazy to really progress in the drug game, but he hated feeling like he was leaving his brother out.

"I got you, bruh, just sit tight until the time right," Cordale told him.

"Come on, mane, you been feeding me that same script since y'all started serving y'all own shit. If you not gone fuck with me, just say that, bruh… don't keep spinnin me," Ladale said as a group of women hit the block. Every woman in the crowd looked good, even the worst looking one was fair for a square. Cordale and Willis both considered themselves to be ladies men, so once they saw the group, they barely paid attention to what Ladale was talking about.

"Hold on, mane, let me see what these hoes on," Cordale said, licking his lips before he headed off the porch, followed by Willis. Ladale stood there staring a hole through his brother's back. "What y'all on?" Cordale asked the prettiest woman out the crowd. She was petite, with flawless caramel-colored skin, and long hair flowing down past her shoulders. Cordale stood five-eight and shorty was a few inches taller than him. She had her sexy, long legs showing and he instantly took a liking to her.

"I'm looking for him right there," the petite woman said, pointing past him to Willis, who was standing behind him.

"What's up?" he asked, stepping up.

"You," she replied flirtatiously. "I heard you was throwing a party tonight."

"Hell yeah, y'all tryna come?"

"Yeah, that's why I came through, to give you my number so you can call me and invite me personally."

Cordale watched Willis exchange numbers with the woman he wanted, she was fine as hell and he was going to shoot his shot, until he peeped how she was choosing Willis. Not being one to be around women and not speak, Cordale immediately bucked at one of the other women in the crowd. She went for him, and they exchanged numbers. The whole crew promised to show up at the party before they bought a few bags of weed and left.

When Cordale and Willis made it back to the porch, Ladale had a look on his face Cordale couldn't quite read, it was a mixture of disgust and annoyance.

"What's wrong with you, bruh?" he asked as his pager went off.

"Shit, I'm tryna talk business with you and you tryna chase hoes," Ladale replied angrily.

"We gone talk, bruh, but I just got a page so let me go stand on this nation business," Cordale said, walking down the steps. "We'll talk later on after the party, bruh, just remind me," he said, but Ladale wasn't convinced.

"Aight, let me hold two hundred until later so I can buy me an outfit for the party." He didn't need the money. He was fresh off a lick he'd made a few hundred from, he just wanted to see if he was gone fuck with him or not.

"I don't even got two hundred on me, bruh, it been slow out here," Cordale lied with a straight face. Ladale already owed him some bread and from the looks of it he had no plans of paying him back so letting him borrow more money was out of the question.

"What you got for me then?"

Cordale stopped before making it to his car. Ladale sounded more like he was shaking him down on some Debo shit, than asking for a gapper. He wanted to check him but he didn't, instead he dug in his right pocket and pulled out the money he made off his last serve. "Here," he held the money out, "This all I got on me."

Ladale bopped over to him, grabbed the money out of his hand and stuffed it in his pocket without even counting it. "Good looking bruh," he said to Cordale before shaking up GD with him and heading back to the porch where Willis was twisting up a blunt. "What you on, folks?" Ladale asked him, taking a seat on the steps.

Shit, same ol same ol," Willis replied dryly. He didn't really fuck with Ladale and the feelings were mutual. They weren't beefing but they weren't friends either.

Willis felt like he was scary and hid behind his brother. He had a big mouth but when shit hit the fan, he always ran to Cordale with his problems. If it weren't for Cordale, Willis wouldn't even put up with him.

Ladale, on the other hand, felt like Willis envied him for some unknown reason. Deep down, he felt like he was the one always in his brother's ear about him, he felt like that's what was holding him back from putting him on. Though he would never admit it, Ladale was jealous of Willis' relationship with his brother. Willis was way closer to Cordale than he was. If you didn't know any better, you would've thought Willis was Cordale's blood and Ladale was just the friend. All the brotherly things Cordale used to do with him, he now did with Willis.

He was a few years older than Cordale, so at first Ladale thought maybe he was outgrowing his younger brother, but then reality set in, and he saw his little brother was actually outgrowing him. Cordale was more respected, more well-known in the streets, he was making more money and fucking prettier women than Ladale was. He tried not to hate on his brother, but he couldn't help it. He hated Willis even more though, he felt like it should've been him on Cordale's side.

"What, you niggas grabbing now, like three pounds apiece?" Ladale asked.

Willis was quiet for a second while contemplating his answer. He didn't know if Cordale wanted him to know what he was copping and not only that, but he didn't want Ladale watching his pockets. "That new whip set me back, so I only had enough to cop me a half a pound. I don't know what Dale copped doe," he lied.

"Front me a zip."

It took everything in Willis to keep him from laughing in Ladale's face. He knew by "front," Ladale really meant give him a zip to smoke up, and then lie about what happened to the money when it was time for him to pay up. "I can't even do it. I told you that whip knocked a patch out my pockets," Willis said before flaming up his blunt.

"Man, you niggas be acting tight as hell, like y'all don't wanna see me eating too," Ladale gruffed. "Aye G, let's rob this petty ass nigga," he told O Dog, shaking up GD with him.

"The only thing you niggas gone take from me is advice," Willis shot back after exhaling a lungful of smoke.

"Yeah, whatever. You don't even have a gun on you, so how you gone stop us?" Ladale asked standing up.

"Who don't have a gun?" Willis asked, flashing the butt of his Smith and Wesson .38.

Ladale mugged Willis for a few seconds before his frown flipped over into a small smile. "That's why I love this nigga, G," he said, looking over at O Dog. "He be ready for whatever," he said with a chuckle, but Willis didn't find anything funny. He took his threat personal but didn't react, because he knew he was more bark than bite. "Let me hit the weed," Ladale said, reaching out until Willis passed him the blunt.

"Y'all can have that. I got a few moves to make, I'm bout to get up outta here," Willis told Ladale and O Dog before walking to his car, hopping in and pulling off.

"Why you be playing with Lil Willis like that, folks?" O dog asked Ladale after plucking the blunt from his fingertips.

"I was just talking shit. That soft ass nigga thought I was for real doe, didn't he mane?"

O Dog shrugged and hit the blunt.

"How much you think he sitting on?" Ladale asked.

"Probably a pound and a few thousand. That nigga be stacking his paper, but you know he a go all out when they throw them parties, so he probably ain't holding right now."

"Same shit I was thinking," Ladale replied. They rotated the blunt in silence for a few minutes before he asked, "Is them niggas still coppin from Lil Wesley?" "Hell yeah, and he been taxin they ass, because he mad they doing they own thing, instead of working for him. He tryna make sure they stay dependent on him."

"That's some ol hatin ass shit."

"His bitch ass... we should hit his crib and see what we could come up on."

"On the boss, we should," O Dog agreed with a smile. He was just as grimy as Ladale was. He was originally from 69th and Racine, but he had family on 47th so the block was like his second home.

***

Two hours later, they were standing at Lil Wesley's back door, trying to pick his lock. Lil Wesley and his bitch shared a crib on the block, and since everybody from the hood knew each other and were so close, Ladale and O Dog had to wear masks to conceal their identities. After five minutes of Ladale unsuccessfully trying to pick the lock, O Dog took a few steps back and kicked the door, knocking it off the hinges.

"Look at all the noise you making, stupid ass nigga!" Ladale gruffed, rushing into the crib. They immediately ran to Lil Wesley's room on the second story of the home. Ladale ram shacked the closet, while O Dog rummaged through the dresser drawers. "Here go a few pounds!" Ladale told O Dog, tossing a black bookbag on Lil Wesley's bed. He was disappointed when he didn't find any more weed. "Wasn't shit in them drawers?" he asked, while checking pillowcases before flipping over the mattress on the bed.

"Hell naw," O Dog said, quickly snatching the .9mm that was under the mattress. They quickly searched the rest of the room before they heard the front door open and close. "Shit, somebody just came in," O Dog said, upping the .9 he'd just found and chambering a round.

"Shhhh," Ladale hushed him putting a finger to his lips before pulling out the .380 he was carrying. He already had one up top, so he didn't have to cock it back. He tiptoed out of the room and down the stairs. Once he was halfway down the stairs, a skinny brown-skinned guy, with long cornrows came out of the kitchen heading for the stairs. It was Lil Wesley.

"What the fu—" Lil Wesley reached for the .40 he had on his waist but before he could get it all the way out, Ladale sent three shots his way, making him dive behind his leather sofa. Ladale bolted down the stairs and Lil Wesley popped up, blowing his .40, bullets smacked the wall behind Ladale's head, knocking chunks of drywall out of the wall. Ladale threw his arm back and squeezed his trigger. He made it to the kitchen and out of the back door.

Once outside, he ran like a bat outta hell. It took a minute or two before he realized he was alone. The mask he had on had him hot, but he kept it on until he was a few blocks away. He had his car parked on 46th and Ellis, he was walking so fast he made it there in less than two minutes. Ladale drove around, looking for O Dog for an hour, before giving up and pulling up on the block. It was close to fifty people standing in front of Lil Wesley's house.

Ladale parked, lit up a Newport, hopped out and walked to where Cordale and Willis were standing. "What the fuck going on, bruh?" he asked, seeing Cordale's tearstained face. Willis, along with everybody else who was out there, had wet faces.

"Somebody ran in Lil Wesley's spot and killed him," Cordale replied, wiping tears from his eyes. He was crushed, Lil Wesley was his big homie, the man who taught him everything he knew about the weed game and gave him his first jab to sell.

"Damn man, don't tell me that," Ladale said somberly, dropping his head, feigning sadness. "When that shit happen?"

"Like an hour ago."

Ladale put his hand over his face, took a deep breath and forced a few tears out of his eyes. If somebody was filming him, he would've won an Oscar for the performance he was putting on. When Cordale came closer to him to pat his back in an attempt to console him, he snatched away and stomped off to his car. Once inside, he had to laugh at his antics, he knew he was doing a good job at putting it on thick.

After a few minutes, Cordale came to the car and knocked on the window. "You good, bruh?" he asked after Ladale rolled down the window.

"Hell naw, I'm not good?" he replied in a low tone. "That nigga Wes was one of the realest niggas I knew," he added. he almost made himself laugh because he called Lil Wesley, "Wes." No one called him that.

"You ain't lying, mane. I almost want to cancel the party tonight."

"Naw don't do that, you know folks would've wanted us to party in his memory, instead of being out here all sad and shit."

"You think he had some weed in his crib?" "Shit if he did the police gone find that shit. I wish we could've emptied his shit out before they got inside," Ladale said. Cordale shot him a funny look that he caught. "That shit ain't no good in the police hands. At least we could've sold some of that shit and helped pay for his funeral," he added, quickly cleaning up what he said at first.

"Yeah, you right," Cordale said before his pager went off. It was the woman he pulled earlier that day. "I'm bout to go get dressed for the party. I'll see you later, bruh."

"A'ight mane," Ladale said, sticking his hand out the window to shake up with him.

"Be safe, bruh, I love you."

"I love you too, mane," Ladale said before starting up his car and pulling off. He wanted to search for O Dog a little more before going to get dressed for the party.

***

When Ladale walked into the house on 47th and Vincennes, where the party was being held, he immediately forgot about Lil Wesley and O Dog and began searching for potential robbery candidates. Where he lacked in hustling, he made up for in his ability to lure people in and rob them blind. He was a good stick-up kid when he was drunk, and with someone he wanted to prove a point to.

The party had started thirty minutes ago and was already live and in full effect. Hoes were all over the room dancing and shaking ass to the Uncle Luke song playing loudly throughout the home.

Ladale walked past a few of the Black Stones from 45th and Cottage Grove. They weren't into it with the Moes, but he didn't like them, especially the ones his age he used to fight in his high school days. One of the Moes he knew as Nard nodded towards him, and he gave him a slight nod. He spotted Cordale, along with Willis and Willis' younger brother Winky, entertaining a group of women by the kitchen. He made his way through the crowded party until he was stopped by someone grabbing his shoulder.

"Let me go!" he gruffed, snatching away to turn around and see one of the BD's from the Calumet Buildings named Big Deon standing there with a few of his boys.

"What's the word, folks?" Ladale asked him, softening his tone.

"What's up with that bread you owe me, skud?" Big Deon asked with a mug on his face.

"What bread?"

"Don't play with me, skud. I fronted you a zip of hard and I haven't heard from you since then." Ladale knew exactly what he was talking about but he ran his hand over his goatee and acted like he was deep in thought.

"I thought we been situated that lil situation," he lied.

"Hell naw, nigga. I haven't seen or heard from you since then, so what's up? What you got for me?"

"I'm fucked up right now but give me a few days and pull up on me on the Seven and I got you," Ladale said as Cordale walked up. He saw the tension in Big Deon's face from across the room, that's what made him walk over.

"What's up, bruh?" he asked while mugging the BD's.

"Shit just rotating with my boy Big D, he was just asking about one of the hoes in here," Ladale lied. "We all good... right, B?"

"Yeah," Big Deon agreed with a nod. "I'ma get up with you in a few days fasho," he said before walking off. He had enough respect for Cordale to give Ladale a pass and not ruin everyone's night.

When the BD s walked off Ladale checked Cordale out in his Cross Colors outfit with a pair of Retro Jordan 4's. "Look at yo fresh ass, mane," he joked.

"I try, I try," Cordale joked wiping imaginary dust off his shoulders.

"This bitch jumping tonight, look at all the hoes in here," Ladale said, scanning the room, admiring the variety of women who were in attendance.

Throwing parties was just one of Cordale's many hustles, he charged five dollars at the door and sold weed and cups of liquor. he usually raked in no less than twenty-five hundred when he threw a party. He was very popular. He never played sports or excelled academically, but his personality made him stand out and shine brighter than his school's star point guard, and the starting quarterback. They looked like lames standing next to him. He kept himself fresh, always clad in the latest fashion. His shoe game was so superb you would've thought he was endorsed by Nike.

Everybody knew he was making money and they also knew he was a gangster by every definition of the word. Everybody either knew him or they heard of him. That's why his parties were a must. He never hosted a weak party. Ladale had to admit he fucked plenty of bitches just because he was Cordale's brother. He was positive he would be leaving tonight's party with some pretty bitch, it always ended like that.

"You surprised by that?" Cordale asked cockily.

"Not at all bruh. So, what's up with that business we was talking about earlier?"

Cordale screwed up his face. "Chill bruh, I got you, don't even worry about that shit right now. Just enjoy the party."

"Aight, G." Ladale smiled and shook up with his brother before going to post up in a dark corner to observe the scenery. He peeped one of the Mafia Insane Vice Lords from the 4120 Building, entertaining a few women on the other side of the room. The guy was CB, he was getting big money and it looked like he was in the party alone. If so, then Ladale was going to try his luck at robbing him. He was sure he had at least a couple thousand on him, and probably some work.

While watching CB like a hawk, he noticed the group of women who had come through the block earlier to enter the party. They were all dressed in short, sexy dresses that screamed, "I want to get fucked!" The women wandered around the party until they found Cordale, Willis and their crowd. Cordale hugged the thick, dark-skinned woman while Willis ran game on the beautiful petite woman that chose him earlier that day. The hoes were smiling and blushing like they were talking to a couple celebrities.

Ladale made his way over to where they were. "Aye Dale, let me see yo cellphone real quick," he asked his brother while checking out a few of the women. Cordale pulled out his phone and handed it to him, he went upstairs to the bathroom where it was slightly quieter than the rest of the house. He dialed O Dog's number and after three unsuccessful attempts, he finally got an answer.

"Hello?" an elderly woman answered.

"Hey, Ms. B, is Romeo in?"

"Yes, but he's sleeping right now," O Dog's mother replied.

"This Ladale and I really need to talk to him, it's very important, so could you please wake him up for me?"

Ms. B smacked her lips and then the line went silent for a couple of minutes.

"Hello?" O Dog said sleepily.

"Damn G, what the fuck happened?" Ladale asked.

O Dog was silent was silent for a minute until he finally realized who he was speaking to. "What you mean, 'What the fuck happened?' You killed Lil Wesley, and I got the fuck outta there!" he replied.

"I killed him?" Ladale asked softly. He felt his chest tighten and his heart started thumping hard in his chest. He felt like he was about to have a heart attack. He thought O Dog had taken Lil Wesley out while he was focused on him.

"On the G, folks, I never even shot."

"Aight, so where them pounds at?"

"I left that shit there. I was so fucked up in the head when I seen Lil Wesley laying there dead, I dropped everything and ran."

"So, you left the pounds?" Ladale asked, twisting up his face. He couldn't believe what he was hearing.

"Hell yeah, I panicked, folks."

Ladale knew a lie when he was hearing one and if O Dog could see the expression on his face, he would've known that he knew he was lying. "So, what about the gun you grabbed? I need that."

"The gun was in the bookbag with the pounds G and I dropped the bookbag as I was running out."

"G, who the fuck you think you talking to?" Ladale asked raising his voice. "You better have something for me or I'ma smoke yo ass, just like I smoked Lil Wesley!" he shouted before hanging up in O Dog's face. Ladale wasn't normally the tough guy type, he hung with the tough guys, but he only did that because it was beneficial.

He was grimy but he wasn't a murderer. He was a thief not a shooter. When he killed Lil Wesley, that wasn't intentional. He was only shooting at him to get him off his ass so he could make it out of the home. The thought of catching his first body had him feeling empowered, the only reason why he was talking to O Dog so crazy, he was feeling himself.

When Ladale walked out of the bathroom, a pretty brown-skinned woman was standing there, she tried to turn away and walk off when he swung the door open.

"You was tryna get in here?" he asked.

"Yes, but I could use the one in the basement," she replied quickly. She kept her eyes down like she was scared to look at him.

"Naw, you good," he said, moving out of her way. She quickly slid in the bathroom and shut the door. Ladale stood there wondering if she had overheard any of his conversation. Moments later when the woman came out of the bathroom, he was still standing right there, and she bumped into him. He could see fear all in her eyes.

"You good, right?" he asked and she nodded. "Aight, make sure it stays that way," he told her and walked off.

***

The next morning, Ladale was up and out early, he knew Cordale would be on the block hustling, so he wanted to catch him while it was still early. When he made it on 47th Place, Cordale was indeed standing on their grandmother's porch with Willis and their homie Ed.

"What y'all on?" Ladale asked, shaking up GD with everybody.

"Shit, this nigga Ed just knocked a mufucka out at McDonald's," Willis said with a chuckle.

"Who?"

"Some grown ass nigga that was tryna short me on some paper," Cordale spoke up.

"Speaking of paper, what's up with that business?" Ladale asked, rubbing his hands together. Cordale reached in the mailbox, grabbed a Ziploc bag containing some weed and handed it to him.

"What's this?" he asked, frowning at the weed.

"Willis suggested that we start you off with an ounce just so you can get yo line going."

Ladale cut his eyes at Willis. If looks could kill, he would've been lifeless.

"An ounce ain't shit, bruh, y'all could've hit me with a QP or something," he complained.

"Beggars can't be choosers!" Willis snapped. "You acting ungrateful as hell, folks. That ain't a good look," he said with a mug on his face. He wasn't Cordale, he never held his tongue when it came to Ladale.

"Don't get me wrong, folks. I'm grateful but I'm just saying I can handle more than what y'all giving me."

"Aight, well get that shit off and come back with one-twenty-five, stop bitchin and complaining and shit. On the G, that shit irritating as hell."

"I'm not Winky, nigga, watch how you handle me," Ladale shot back.

"Shit, we all know you not Winky, that's obvious," Willis said with a chuckle.

"Fuck that supposed to mean?"

"It mean you and Winky cut from two different cloths and everybody can see that."

Ladale took a deep breath and ran his hand over his face. "So, what you sayin, bruh?"

"He ain't sayin shit, bruh, leave that shit alone," Cordale intervened, seeing things were about to spiral out of control. "You got the weed it, shouldn't matter how much it is, as long as we gave you some rhythm. That's the only thing that should matter. Flip that shit, and let's run this bag up," Cordale was saying right before his cell phone rang. He answered, had a brief conversation and hung up. "I got some shit to handle. Willis, ride with me," he said, before turning to his brother who was standing there mugging Willis. "You good, bruh?" he asked.

"Yeah," he replied dryly. They shook up and Ladale stormed off to his car.

Thirty minutes later, Ladale was with one of his freaks, hitting her from the back while holding the back of her neck. "Who pussy is this," he asked, watching his dick slam in and out of her fat pussy.

"It's yours," the woman purred seductively.

"If it's my pussy, why were you all in that nigga's face?" Ladale asked, picking up the pace of his strokes. He was trying to punish her tight pussy.

"Because you told me to be like that."

"But it looked like you was really feelin that nigga."

"No... no... no... baby," the woman cried in ecstasy.

"You gone make sure I get that nigga, right?"

"Yes daddy," the woman answered. Ladale flipped her over and climbed on top of her. He slid his hard dick inside of her, grabbed one of her big breasts and hungrily sucked on her nipple. He hit her with slow, passionate strokes, until he was squirting his seed inside of her. He then kissed her lips a few times before rolling off of her.

"What's up with yo cousin? She still in, right?" he asked, trying to catch his breath.

"Yes, I told you that a million times," the woman snapped.

"Did she say anything to you about me?"

"No, Ladale. What would she have to say to me about you?"

"Nothing, I was just asking, baby," Ladale replied with a smile. He had a master plan in motion and in order for it to work, he needed his little freak and her cousin to come through. He was giving her all of his time and money, eating her pussy, sucking her toes and giving her grade-A dick to make sure she stuck to the plan and did what she had to do. If he didn't love her now, she would most definitely have all of his love when everything was said and done.

Thinking about his plan coming into fruition made his dick hard. He got up and climbed between the freak's legs, he planned on licking her pussy until she begged for him to stop and then give her another round of sex, she deserved it.

Molotti

Chapter 6

Blake, Von D, and one of the BD's named Lil Hot were riding around in a stolen Chevy Malibu. They were riding through an area on the east side of the city called "Bush," looking for a Latin King to kill. The Kings ran Bush. They had just gotten a call that King Ice had come through the hood shooting. Once they got on 84th and Buffalo, Blake, who was driving, pulled over on the corner of the block and let Lil Hot out.

"You walk up on they ass and we gone pop up from the other end," Blake instructed, popping the locks.

"Aight," Lil Hot replied with a nod before climbing out of the car and heading down Buffalo. It was a crowd of Latinos posted in the middle of the block. Blake pulled off as Lil Hot headed for the crowd.

Blake drove to 83rd street and put his car in neutral. He grabbed his Glock 20 and hopped out. Von D was right behind him, clutching his Glock 30. They marched to the corner of Buffalo. When they rounded the corner, they bumped into three Latinos, who were walking and shit talking. Blake quickly upped the Glock he held in his hand and fired shots. Von D followed suit. The Latinos tried to run but the duo was all over them. The three men all dropped and that's when they heard a couple other guns going off and they took off running for their car.

Blake whipped the car out of its spot and flew around the block to where they had dropped Lil Hot off. When he pulled on the corner, he saw Lil Hot running their direction being hawked down by two Latin Kings. One King was shooting a .9 and the other was shooting a .40 with both hands. Lil Hot must've gotten hit, because he fell but quickly got up. Blake stomped the gas and sped off.

"What you doing?" Von D asked him.

"Man, they was all over his ass. They can have one, but it wasn't no way in hell I was about to sit right there and let them kill all three of us," Blake replied, navigating through traffic. Lil Hot was one of the folks, but he wasn't in his immediate circle. As far as he was concerned, he was just another pawn on his chessboard and pawns were disposable, they were meant to die for the King.

Von D kept his eyes on his mirror, but occasionally peeked over at Blake. He couldn't comprehend how he had just left one of his mans for dead and was now bobbing his head to Lil Durk like nothing had just happened. That was some cold shit. Von didn't really know Lil Hot like that, but he felt bad for leaving him. "Drop me off to my whip I got a few moves to make," he told Blake. He really did have some business to attend to but that wasn't the reason why he was trying to get away from Blake. He didn't like the stunt he had just pulled, it really had him wondering if KD was right about all the backdoor shit he was saying about him.

***

Mo Money sat in Bang's passenger seat texting his baby mother, he should've been watching his mirrors for any signs of them being followed or for twelve, but he wasn't too much worried about either. Bang was nice behind the wheel, plus he had just bought the Volkswagen they were in, so nobody knew the car.

"Let's slide through 79th and 83rd and see if we could catch something," he suggested, not looking up from his phone. He wanted to cash in on the contracts Chito had on the niggas from over there.

"Aight. I gotta slide through the hood and grab my lil cousin first," Bang replied. They drove listening to G Herbo's latest mixtape while rotating exotic stuffed woods. Mo Money was so engulfed in his text messages that he didn't pay attention to the fact Bang was being unnaturally quiet. He would usually be talking shit if he wasn't rapping along to the music. Mo Money looked over at him and saw the frustration through the wrinkles in his forehead. "What's up with you, Law?" he asked.

"If a mufucka was to put a bag on my head, like a real bag like that half a million, would you cash me in?" Bang asked.

Mo Money thought about it for a few seconds before answering.

"Naw, not you," he replied, not looking over at Bang.

"Man, you frontin yo shit!" Bang said, before erupting in laughter. His laughter was so contagious that even though he didn't want to, Mo Money joined him and started cracking up.

"On Stone, I would think about it fasho, but I wouldn't do it. You one of the only niggas I can trust out here," Mo Money replied laughing. Still, he had discreetly put his phone down and grabbed his gun, acting like he was looking through the mirrors on point. The question had really thrown him off and had him feeling like it had a hidden message behind it. Niggas didn't ask shit like that for no reason.

"I'm one of the only niggas you can trust?" Bang asked in disbelief. His smirk showed he didn't believe it. When the fuck did you start trusting anybody?" he asked.

"Oh, I trust you," Mo Money replied quickly. "I just trust you to a certain extent," he said, staring into the mirror as if he was watching the traffic. But he was really watching Bang, who he knew was just as cutthroat as he was. He wasn't scared at all. He was really ready to empty his clip in Bang if he made the wrong move. The only reason he had survived this long was because he acted first and thought about it later.

"What if you had half a million on you, do you think I would cash you in?" Bang asked. The question made Mo Money tighten the grip he had on his Glock; he was almost starting to feel like that was the case.

"I don't know, you probably would, you probably wouldn't," he replied with a shrug "But if you tried and fucked up, you know that's yo ass, right?" he asked with a sinister smirk on his face.

"I know how you comin, Moe," Bang agreed with a nod. "But you know how I get when I want a mufucka gone. You remember how I did Nell. I shot his whole fuckin face off," he said, smiling at the memory.

"I called that play. Do you remember how I did dude over east?

"Which one?"

"The Nigga from Dro City?"

"Aw, yeah. On my sister, you did him dirty," Bang replied, parking his car in front of the Courtway Building on 61st and Kimbark. They got out the car and headed into one of the hallways of the building. In the hallway, a few men were standing around talking shit while rotating Backwoods. In the laundry room, a few men were having a dice game.

"What y'all shooting?" Mo Money asked, pulling out a wad of money. He was an avid gambler.

"Hundreds, you broke ass nigga," a brown-skinned dreadhead with tatts on his face said. The guy was Mo Money's older cousin, Sheed. The hood they were in was a hood called CrankTown, run by the Black Stones. Mo Money had a lot of family from the area.

"I won't be broke after I break y'all sweet ass," Mo Money said, before trying to place a side bet. Bang shook his head at how easily distracted he could be.

"Aye Money, we on something right now, you can shoot later," Bang said. Mo Money held up a finger and after the guy who was on the dice crapped out, he followed Bang to an apartment on the third floor. Bang beat on the door and seconds later, a dreadhead swung it open.

"What the fuck you beating on the door like that for? You trippin bruh!" the dreadhead snapped. The diamonds in his mouth sparkled and shined with every word he spoke. He was shirtless, showing off his tatted-up torso, every inch of his skin was covered in ink.

"Shut yo bitch ass up," Bang retorted, brushing past him into the apartment followed by Mo Money. "You ready to get out here with me?" Bang asked, picking up a Glock .44 that was sitting on the living room table and looking at it in disgust. "And who weak ass gun is this?" he asked, holding the gun with two fingers like it was infectious.

"Watch yo mouth, bruh, and that's my pops gun," the dreadhead replied snatching the gun from Bang. He kept looking at Mo Money who seemed to look vaguely familiar to him. "You ever been to Memphis?" he asked him.

"Hell naw," Mo Money replied flatly.

"Mo Money, this my lame ass, country ass cousin, Domo. You probably seen him around here before he moved outta town. This Lumps' son," Bang said.

"You from the Crank?" Domo asked.

"Naw, I'm from the Hundreds, Risky Road, but I been around here all my life. My whole family from down here."

"Who yo family?"

"Panda, Sheed, Lil Johnny, Killa Key, Chico—"

"I know moe nem, you look familiar as hell doe, bruh," Domo told Mo Money before turning back to Bang. "Cuz, I really need to find this bitch before it's too late and she spend all my mufuckin paper or get finessed outta all the shit she stole from me," he said. He was only in Chicago, in pursuit of his ex-girlfriend, who had stolen a lot of money and enough drugs to make a few people rich. It was some powerful people tied up in that money and drugs, and if he couldn't replace the money or come up with the product, he was fucked. His father told him that if anybody could find the bitch, it was Bang.

"Do you know who she out here with?" Bang asked Domo, grabbing a half-smoked wood out of a glass ashtray that sat on the coffee table.

"I think she out here with her pops, but I'm not sure. As far as I know that bitch didn't even know her real daddy, but that's who I heard she ran to."

"So, you don't know his name, where he from or what side of the city she could be on?"

"Hell naw."

"We can ask around and see if it's a bitch from outta town out here making moves. I'm sure she'll stand out, you Memphis mufuckas country as hell," Mo Money said.

"She stole some Percs, Xans and Viagras, so when you ask around you should ask if it's a bitch that got a lot of that shit."

"How she look?" Mo Money asked, and Domo pulled out his phone and showed him a picture. "Aw yeah, I would fuck the shit outta her lil chocolate ass," he said, licking his lips.

"Let me see," Bang said, jumping up from where he was seated.

"Yeah, she slight," he agreed, looking through her pictures.

"A bitch with a lot of pills shouldn't be hard to find at all. In the meantime, let's go kill somebody," Bang insisted, tossing Domo his shirt.

**

Cordale stared at Ladale with annoyance written all over his face. He had just wasted his last few hours, telling him a story that answered none of his questions, or gave him any type of closure.

"What does Lil Wesley, or O Dog, or any of that shit you just told me got to do with you killing TayTay?" he asked calmly.

"It's more to the story, bruh, just listen," Ladale said before going back to his story.

Summer 1996

After Lil Wesley got killed, 47th Place was free enterprise when it came to weed. The only problem for Cordale and Willis was, they didn't have a plug who would give them the weed at the price Lil Wesley was giving it to them for, and still throw them something on consignment.

Ladale sold the ounce they had given him quickly, in hopes they would hit him off with something bigger than an ounce, but they gave him another ounce and told him to keep up the good work. He blamed it all on Willis. Somewhere in his mind, he thought Willis was hating on him, for what reason he didn't know, but he hated the influence he had over his brother. They were both pushing new whips, wearing gold chains and fucking the prettiest bitches, while he was still pushing his old ass hoopty, fucking hoodrats. It was almost as if they didn't want to see him shining like they were.

A fine ass, light-skinned woman he'd seen around from time to time walked up, breaking his train of thought. "Hey Cordale," she purred, giving Cordale a tight hug. "Hey, Willis. Hey..." she said to Ladale last, not addressing him by his name, maybe because she didn't know it.

*"What's up TayTay?" Cordale asked cooly.
"Nothing much, just came to check you out for a minute,"
TayTay replied with a smile, showing her perfect teeth. Ladale
raised a brow as he watched the two interact. He remembered the
woman for being all over Willis, now it seemed as if Cordale had
her attention. If she was going like that, then he was going to shoot
his shot next. Cordale and TayTay left off the porch to go sit in his
car and smoke a blunt. Ladale watched them interact while selling
his nickel bags. He was glad she had Cordale's attention because
he was getting most of the serves that came through.*

*This nickel and diming wouldn't do it though, he wanted to
serve weight. Ladale cut his eyes towards Willis, who was sitting on
his porch with one of TayTay's friends named Sade. He started
imagining it was Willis he had robbed and killed, instead of Lil
Wesley. As quick as the thought entered his head, it left. He knew
his brother would be crushed if he were to kill Willis. Their motto
was "Loyalty Is Everything," that was cool for them, but if you took
the first letter out of each word and put them together it spelled LIE.
And that's exactly what it was to him. Loyalty was a lie, an illusion
that people used to take advantage of other people who trusted
them. Loyalty wasn't a character trait that he was blessed with, but
he did love his brother, so to keep from hurting him he would keep
his cruel thoughts locked inside the back of his mind. But what he
didn't know was that your thoughts turned into your beliefs, and
your beliefs turned into your actions.*

*Later that night, Ladale got an emergency page from his freak
bitch. He quickly called her up and she filled his ear with some
valuable information. He quickly dressed in all-black, grabbed his
mask, his pistol and rushed out of the house. About ten minutes
later, he was walking through a alley on 46th and Woodlawn. a
rusty gray Ford was sitting at the end of the alley. As he approached
the vehicle from the back, he could see someone was sitting in the
driver's seat. He pulled his ski mask over his face and upped his
gun. When he made it to the driver's side door, he swung it open
and clocked the guy in the head with the butt of his .380.*

"Arghhh!" O Dog yelled, he was in the middle of getting his dick sucked. When the woman, who was sucking his dick looked up and began to scream, Ladale aimed his gun at his face. "Shut the fuck up!" he snapped. His eyes grew big when he recognized the woman. "Where that shit at, nigga?" he asked O Dog, pointing the gun at his chest.

"Ladale, stop playing, folks. I told you I left all that shit when we bussed that move," O Dog said frantically. He purposely said Ladale's name, hoping it would deter him from doing anything crazy. That only pissed him off and made him smack him with the gun again.

"This ain't no Ladale, bitch!" he growled, smacking him again. He saw that O Dog's gun had fallen on the floor and he quickly snatched it up. "Where that weed at, bruh?" he asked.

"Ladale, you and yo brother the only two country mufuckas in the hood, so I know it's you behind that mask, G." Ladale knew he was busted, so he started to panic. "Bitch, get out and run as far as you can, without stopping or looking back," he told the woman, who got out the car and bolted through the alley. "Aight, bitch nigga, you know it's me so you should know I'm not playing. Where the fuck them pounds at?" he told O Dog.

"G, I told you I left—"

BOW! BOW!

Ladale shot him twice in his leg. O Dog began howling in pain while gripping his thigh. Ladale watched as his thick blood oozed through his fingers. "Don't make me smoke you, bruh."

"G, how many times do I have to tell you I don't have that shit?" O Dog said through clenched jaws. "Folks, you know you done fucked up by shooting me," he added threateningly. He was right and Ladale knew it. O Dog was going to fuck him up behind this stunt. He was really like that, so Ladale couldn't give him a chance to catch him slipping, so he raised his gun and fired three shots. Two hit O Dog in his neck and one hit him in his eye. Blood squirted out of each hole. Ladale stood there watching for a few seconds, before bolting through the alley.

***

Present Day

"So, let me guess. TayTay was the woman in the car sucking O Dog's dick?" Cordale asked and Ladale nodded slowly. "So you killed my son's mother because you got caught up doing same grimy ass shit? You could've came to me, you know I could've made her be quiet. Was she threatening you with going to the police or something?" he asked, feeling his anger rise.
"Let me finish, bruh," Ladale replied through chapped lips.

***

Spring 1997

Cordale fell in love with TayTay quickly. She was everything he wanted in a woman. Loyal, honest, faithful, beautiful and trustworthy. Not only that, but she had helped him elevate in the drug game by introducing him to her older cousin Shaw, who was the weed connect he so desperately needed. The only thing that stopped were him and Willis getting weed on consignment. They only took fronts from Lil Wesley because he was like family, but they barely knew Shaw and they both knew when you were selling drugs, anything could happen at any moment. So, to eliminate bullshit before it happened, they always paid for their pounds upfront.

Ladale was still hustling; he was now up to a half a pound at a time. He would've been grabbing more but he spent his money as quick as he made it. He always wanted a new pair of shoes or a new outfit and every day, he wanted to drink and smoke with the neighborhood freaks. He walked and talked as if he was the man, and his pockets suffered the consequences of him trying to keep up with that facade.

On this particular night, Cordale and Willis were throwing a pajama party the whole hood had been talking about. They were still throwing some of the craziest parties and this one was sure to be one for the ages. The party started at 9:00 pm and Ladale entered, wearing a blue and white plaid pajama fit with a pair of Air Max 95's to match. His small gold chain swung from his neck as he bopped through the party, checking out all the pretty women who were in attendance. Cordale, Willis, Ed and Winky were all in the kitchen, wearing custom-made Gucci robes with their names stitched in the backs. Every one of them looked like they were getting money. They each carried their own bottle of champagne.

Ladale always felt left out when they did shit like that and "forgot" to add him. He knew he wasn't really a part of their crew, they just dealt with him because he was Cordale's big brother. Little did they know, he really didn't give a fuck. He had his own homies and one day soon, he would be the head of his own crew.

Halfway through the party, TayTay and another woman started fighting over Cordale. TayTay had seen them dancing together and that didn't sit well with her, so she approached the woman, and all hell broke loose. "Take TayTay to the crib for me bruh," Cordale told Ladale after they broke the fight up.

"I'm not going anywhere if you're not going with me!" TayTay slurred. She had drunk way too many Long Island Ice Tea's and was beyond tipsy.

"You know I gotta stay here and make my money."
"Willis can handle it."

"TayTay not here, not now," Cordale said firmly, stepping in her face. "Go yo ass home and I'll be there soon," he said, and she stormed off.

"You straight?" Ladale asked TayTay once they were inside his car. She had her arms folded over her chest, staring out of her window.

"Yeah," she mumbled after a few seconds.

"That nigga was wild for having shorty all over him knowing you right there."

"Tell me about it."

"Bruh be doing some dumb ass shit," Ladale said, but TayTay didn't respond. He picked up his cup of Hennessy, drank a little and

handed her the cup. "Kill that shit then flame up the blunt in the ashtray, you look like you need to get high," he said.

TayTay downed the cup and then lit the blunt as instructed. They smoked in silence until they pulled up to Cordale's duplex. TayTay stumbled on her way up the stairs and Ladale caught her. He let his hand linger on her ass for a while before letting go. Once inside, she rushed up the stairs and closed their bedroom door. Twenty minutes later, she came stumbling out of the room holding a bookbag. She was mumbling something about bitch ass niggas. When she got through the dark living room and almost to the front door, she was startled by Ladale speaking.

"Where you going?" he asked. He was sitting on the couch in the dark.

TayTay flicked on the living room's light. "I-I didn't know you was still here," she stammered. Ladale noticed that something was off about her.

"Where you going?" he asked again.

"T-to Sade house."

"I thought Cordale told you to chill here until he made it home."

"Fuck him, he not my daddy," she spat, watching Ladale get up and close the space between them. The way his eyes hungrily ran over her body made her kind of uncomfortable. Even though the alcohol had her mind cloudy, she could see the lust in his eyes.

"What's in that bag?" he asked, taking his eyes off her thighs to look at the bag she was carrying.

"Some clothes," she lied.

Ladale could look at the bookbag and see that it was too flat to be stuffed with clothes, so he yanked it off her shoulder with so much force that she almost fell. He unzipped the bookbag and smiled at what he saw. "You dirty bitch!" he said, coldly pulling his .380 off his waist. TayTay had three pounds and a few wads of money in the bookbag, which he was sure belonged to his brother. "My brother does everything for yo stankin ass and you stealing from him?" he asked with a scowl on his face.

TayTay's eyes grew large. She was one person who knew Ladale's secret of killing O Dog, so she used that as her ace. "Ok, you got me, but I know that that was you who killed O Dog. He said your name and I remember your voice. If you don't say anything about this, I won't say nothing about what you did," she said, causing him to erupt in laughter.

"If you know that was me, then you should know I killed O Dog because he knew it was me. That's the only reason I killed him. You catching my drift?" he asked with a wicked grin.

TayTay caught on immediately and began to plead for her life. "Please, Ladale... it's not that serious."

"Yes, it is. If you'll steal, ain't no telling what else you would do. What's Cordale's favorite saying?" Ladale looked up to the ceiling as if he was thinking. "Loyalty Is Everything. And you not even loyal."

"I'm sorry, just tell me what I could do to keep this between us."

"You shouldn't be worried about me keeping a secret, you should be worried about keeping your life."

"Ok. Ok... please, Ladale. I'll do anything," TayTay cried.

"Show me," Ladale challenged.

"How?" she asked with tears in her eyes.

"For starters, let a nigga see what that head do," Ladale said, licking his lips.

"Nigga, you got me fucked all the way up!" TayTay snapped, frowning her pretty face up.

"Or you could get shot the fuck up, hoe," Ladale threatened, mean mugging her.

She could see the seriousness in his dark, evil eyes so she defeatedly dropped to her knees and pulled his hard dick out of his pajama pants and boxers. Her stomach churned and she could feel the bile rising in the back of her throat. What he was making her do, had her sick to her stomach literally. She had to force herself to put the head of his dick in her mouth.

"I can't do it," she said with tears dripping from her eyes. Ladale didn't reply, he simply put the barrel of his gun to her head and that was enough to persuade her to suck it up and give him what he wanted. TayTay closed her eyes tightly and pretended that it was

Cordale's dick she was holding. That helped her relax a little and she began to suck Ladale's dick, making him moan, groan and stand on his tippy toes.

He grabbed the back of her head and forced his dick all the way down her throat, making her gag. The forbidden throat she was giving him was better than any head he'd ever experienced. TayTay was crying when she first started but her tears had ceased, and she was seemingly into it. She was sucking like she enjoyed the taste of Ladale's dick. "Get up and take all that shit off," he demanded.

TayTay got up without a word and stripped of all her clothes. Ladale's eyes roamed her body from her pretty manicured, yellow polished toes, up to her petite thighs, to her neatly trimmed pussy, up to her perky breasts. The sight was heavenly. He had been infatuated with TayTay since the first time he'd seen her. He sat on Cordale's black suede couch and said, "Come here."

TayTay mounted him and when he slid his dick inside of her, he was amazed by how wet she was. He grabbed her by her waist and guided her up and down as she rode his dick. He leaned forward and began to hungrily suck on one of her nipples. That had some type of effect on her because she let a soft moan escape her lips. The alcohol must've been getting the best of her, because when Ladale stopped sucking her titty, she leaned forward and began kissing him on the lips.

They started having passionate sex, Ladale touched all over her body, caressing her as if she was a lost treasure he'd found.

When she came all over his dick, he told her to turn over and she bent over the couch, while he hit her from the back. "Ooooohhh, Ladale, it feel so good," TayTay moaned. Hearing his brother's bitch moaning his name did something to him, it made him fuck her better, like he was trying to prove something to her. When he pulled out and started eating her pussy, she almost started crying, it felt so good.

Cordale had never put his tongue on her, nobody had, so the feeling was new to her, and each time Ladale's tongue swiped her clit, it sent jolts of pleasure through her body. She had an orgasm that made her knees buckle. She couldn't control her breathing. She *fell down on the couch and Ladale was all over her, he entered her from behind and fucked her slowly until he busted a big nut deep inside of her.*

"Now keep that a secret and I'll keep yours," Ladale told TayTay, kissing the nape of her neck. It surprised him when she turned her head and began kissing him on the lips.

***

Present Day

Cordale was trembling with anger while listening to Ladale tell his story. He couldn't believe what he was hearing. None of it added up to him. "So, you raped TayTay?" he asked in disgust.

"It wasn't rape, bruh, she wanted to do it just as bad as I did," Ladale replied.

"You put a fucking gun to her head, bruh! How isn't that rape?" Cordale asked, standing up. He had his Glock in his hand, ready to kill Ladale, all he saw was red. "So, you killed her because you raped her and you felt like she was going to tell me?"

"No," Ladale said, shaking his head. "We fucked in '97. I didn't kill her until 2010," he added and that gave Cordale something to think about. What happened in those thirteen years to make him kill TayTay? Why hadn't TayTay told him any of this? Those questions kept running through his mind. His anger was slowly dissolving and being replaced with hurt, sadness, pain he was feeling deep within. Maybe Ladale was right about him not being able to handle the truth.

The truth hurt and this shit was overwhelming him. He pulled out a pack of Newports, fished one out and lit it up. "So, it's deeper than the shit you just laid on me, bruh?" he asked after hitting the Newport a few times. Ladale nodded and he took a deep breath. "I can't lie, bruh, this shit almost too much for me to process. My ears can't take no more tonight, so I'll be back first thing in the morning," he said, not attempting to hide the hurt in his voice.

"Aight, bruh. It feel like they been holding me down here for forever, so I guess one more night won't hurt," Ladale replied. He watched Cordale slowly walk off and for the first time in his long life, he felt what he assumed was regret. "Aye, bruh!" he called out. "I'm sorry, bruh," he said when Cordale had made it to the stairs and turned around.

"No, you not," Cordale scoffed. "But you really should be, bruh, I really loved that woman," he said before heading up the stairs, leaving Ladale alone with only the darkness and his thoughts.

Molotti

Chapter 7

Mo Money, Bang and Domo sat outside of one of KD's traps in Princeton Park. They knew KD was inside because his Benz was parked, right in front of the stolen car they were in. They had been sitting in the car for well over an hour and Domo was becoming restless. "Bruh, if we know the nigga inside, what the fuck we doing still sitting in the car? Let's run in that bitch," he said, looking out of the window.

"I was thinking the same shit," Bang agreed. He was wearing a pair of Gucci shades to conceal his red eyes.

"Just chill, man. We don't know what's on the other side of that door, so we gone wait right here until they come out," Mo Money said, not taking his eyes off the crib KD was in. "Can you take that dumb ass grill out yo mouth? It's not hard to point out the dude with the diamond teeth," he added sarcastically.

"This not a grill, this shit permanent, bruh," Domo replied cockily. He didn't too much care for Mo Money, and he could tell the feeling was mutual.

"What made you get that country ass shit and you from Chicago?" Bang asked with a chuckle. He didn't like the grill either.

"Lil Durk and King Von got they mouth bussed down and they from the city," Domo shot back defensively.

"That don't make it cool, or not country," Bang laughed. "I bet yo goofy ass a Blood or a Crip too, ain't you?"

"Fuck outta here, bruh. I'm Big Stone," Domo shot back. "Stop tryna handle me like I'm some sucka ass nigga because I been in Memphis. We get it in too."

Mo Money sighed deeply and shook his head. "Why do every city try to be in competition with Chicago? Y'all must get around us and start feeling soft as hell," he said.

"Don't no nigga make me feel soft. Fuck Chicago!" Domo gruffed. They had his brain.

Before Mo Money could respond, the door to KD's trap swung open and people started pouring out. KD was amongst the last to come out and he was watching the car they were in like a hawk.

When Mo Money saw him nod towards the car, he bounced out with his Glock 22 that was equipped with a drum and a switch. He aimed at KD and tapped the trigger. KD knew what it was when the car door opened, so he grabbed the bitch he had been entertaining and used her as a shield. He felt the bullets slamming into her body as he held her in front of him. One of his guys dropped next to him and he quickly upped his Glock and returned fire.

Bang and Domo hopped out shooting, trading shots with KD and his men. The sound of Domo shooting his Draco made everybody freeze. KD let go of the lifeless bitch he was holding and took off through the cut on the side of the trap. Domo gave chase, he cradled the Draco with two hands, trying to line KD up. He thought since KD was a little chunky, he wouldn't know how to use his legs as well as he did, but he was proven wrong. KD ran through cut after cut, jumping gates and hitting gangways like he had his escape route predetermined. He popped out on 95th and Harvard and hopped into a white Jeep Grand Cherokee that was waiting on him.

A light-skinned guy sitting in the passenger's seat of the Jeep, held a Tech out of the window and sent a flurry of shots at Domo. Domo jumped back in the cut before sticking the Draco out and emptying the rest of the clip at the Jeep, which was speeding off. Domo took off through the alley and found a decent crib to hide behind, until Mo Money and Bang pulled up in the alley to get him.

***

Later that night, Mo Money pulled up to Chito's house and was escorted in by a couple of the King brothers. They knew he was one of the few people Chito allowed in his home with his weapon, so they didn't search him. Chito met him in his living room and offered him a shot of Patrón.

"Where I'm from we don't do shots, we do cups, but I'm straight," Mo Money said, waving the alcohol off.
"So, what's up, Moe man?" Chito asked, taking a seat on his plush couch. He was a very muscular guy and wore his hair slicked back. He looked more Italian than Mexican, but he was full-blooded

Latino.

"I got a few questions I wanted to ask you. I know yo ears hear a lot of things so hopefully, you could help me out." Chito eyeballed Mo Money, studying his facial expression. They'd known each other for years, so he knew nine times out of ten, he was up to no good. He was one of those people you never saw doing good, so you just assumed that he was always up to no good. "I'm listening," Chito said, pouring himself another shot.

"Is there a contract on my head?" Mo Money asked seriously, but the question caught Chito off guard and for some reason made him laugh.

"Is that a trick question?" he asked chuckling, "it's probably been money on your head since before we met."

"I'm not talking about no twenty – fifty thousand, I'm talking about a big bag on my head, a price big enough to make one of my homies cash me in."

"You don't even have friends, Moe. Who you think you foolin, man?" Chito asked, still laughing. He was laughing so hard his face was turning red.

"I think I still got one or two left," Mo Money said seriously with a straight face. Unbeknownst to Chito, he was serious as a heart attack.

"Last I heard, you had a few different prices on your head. Nothing more than a hundred thousand dollars, doe." Chito crossed one leg over the other. "I can put my ear to the streets and find out if you need me to," he said.

"Yeah, if you can put me together a list of everybody who got big contracts on me. I'll sleep better once they're dead."

"I can do that for you, law," Chito said, before knocking back another shot. "How has that other work been going? They usually don't last long once they pop up on your radar. Don't tell me you're getting old on me. You're not the same Risky Road you once was."

"We been doing our homework so we could try to kill three birds with one stone," Mo Money lied. "This contract right here could have me decent for a while, so we're taking our time."

"One of them is working with us giving us information that I've been giving to you, but he's still a liability so that's the only reason he has to go. That and the fact that they killed Iz. I miss my brother," Chito said sadly. "I hate how your people are so easy to betray their morals. It's truly disgusting if you ask me," he said with a frown.

Mo Money frowned too. He didn't like the way he said, *your people*. "I wish I knew which one of them it was so we could kill him in the worst way. Two things I hate are a snake and a rat," he sneered, shaking his head.

"I can't tell you which one it is, but that really doesn't matter because you're going to kill all three of them, right?"

"Facts," Mo Money said before getting up and stretching his small body. "Let me know if you find something out about some money being on me, and don't forget to get that list to me ASAP," he said, extending his hand to Chito to shake up.

"I got you Moe man," Chito said.

***

Suemoo sat in his bedroom at his mother's crib, playing *Grand Theft Auto V*. He was still recovering from when the Latin Kings caught him at Blake's crib and shot him up. He had been in the crib and out of the mix since then. A knock at his front door snatched his attention away from the video game. He got up, grabbed his crutches and maneuvered through his messy room to go answer the door. He looked through the peephole and smiled at the sight of a familiar   face.
"What's the word, gang?" Suemoo asked, swinging the door open for KD.

He hadn't seen any of his friends lately, the only people he saw were the couple women he was fucking on. The smile on Suemoo's face quickly faded when he saw the gun that KD had in his hand. Before he could speak another word, KD lifted his arm and started shooting him in his face at point blank range. Suemoo's body crumbled to the ground, and KD stood over him and pumped a few more shots into his head and body before taking off.

***

When Cordale left from the trap where Ladale was being held, he went straight to the liquor store to grab a fifth of Dussé, before shooting straight to Blake's house. He needed to vent. He needed to be around someone he loved and someone he knew loved him in return. By the time he made it to Blake's crib he had consumed a quarter of the bottle and the liquor was starting to make his head fuzzy.

"What's up, Unc?" Blake asked Cordale, letting him inside his home.

"Hey, Daddy!" Aisha said, sounding like a little girl. She was sitting in the living room rolling up a thick Backwood. Hearing the love in his daughter's greeting was just what Cordale needed. It was crazy because love felt so foreign to him. It'd been so long since he had TayTay and Lil Ced, so sometimes when Aisha showed him the love he so desperately needed, it felt so alien that it scared him.

Cordale plopped down on Blake's sofa and lifted his bottle to his lips. His face told the story of a man who was truly fighting demons. The bags under his eyes and the wrinkles in his forehead were dead giveaways. You would've thought a man who had just beat the feds would be a little happier, but he wasn't.

"What's up, Unc? Talk to me," Blake said, sitting on the loveseat that sat across from the couch. "You must've handled that business," he said. He figured Cordale's mood was off because he had just killed his brother.

"Naw," Cordale replied, shaking his head. "The shit he was laying on me got so heavy that I couldn't listen anymore. I'm still having a hard time processing that shit, mane," he said, taking another gulp from the bottle.

"What he say?" Blake asked, interested in hearing the story. He listened intently as Cordale told him and Aisha what Ladale had told him, almost verbatim. By the end of the story, Cordale was fighting back tears. He had been wanting to cry but he refused to break down in front of Ladale. His pride was too big for that, but in front of

Blake and Aisha he felt vulnerable. Tears started to pour from his eyes in streams.

Aisha rubbed his back while he wept, she wanted to say something to comfort him, but she didn't know what to say. She was glad she never got the chance to meet Ladale. Between her father, Blake and KD, she had heard a lot of stories about him but none were good.

"So now what?" Blake asked after lighting up another wood.

"I'm going back in the morning to let him finish telling his story."

"And after that?" Blake asked, raising a brow.

"He gone get what he got coming," Cordale replied grimly. "He betrayed my trust, he broke our bond, and I lost all the love I had for him when I found out that not only did he kill TayTay, but he instigated a whole war that cost me everything. He gotta die."

"I feel you, Unc."

"When I think about what you and KD got going on, I think of me and Willis. When we fell out, that shit hurt me, he was the last friend I wanted to lose. I just couldn't go against my brother. I was blinded by love and loyalty that didn't exist. It only existed when it was coming from me. Plenty of times I wanted to call Willis up and get that shit figured out, but when you got so many outside forces in yo ear, telling you this and telling you that. It starts to take a toll on you and make you feel like maybe you're the one who's tweaking, because you wanna fix it. Not addressing my problems with Willis like a man, and like I wanted, to cost me a lot. I don't want you and KD going down the same road, because y'all gone be the ones that lose the most. You a grown man, so you gone do what you wanna do, but that's just a little advice from an old man that done seen it all."

"I hear you, Unc, and I love folks to death. I tried to avoid it getting to where it's at now, but it seem like folks got his mind made up," Blake replied, hitting the wood one last time before passing it to Aisha.

"So, would you be willing to squash that shit if he was?"

Blake thought about it for a minute before answering, "Yeah, for the simple fact that we got too much other shit going on, to be into it with each other. I'm not gone front and say that we could ever be how we used to be, but I wouldn't be on his ass if it was up to me."

"I'ma talk to him and see how he feel about it and if we all on the same page we gone have a sit down and get this shit situated. I need y'all more than y'all think," Cordale said, glad to hear Blake was willing to squash the beef.

Blake nodded but the smug look on his face betrayed his nod, he didn't want to sit down with KD. That nigga had shot at him, put dirt on his name and tried to turn the whole hood against him. They were way beyond the point of no return. Even if they did agree to squash it, he didn't trust that KD and Lil Moe wouldn't try to backdoor him.

A call from Blue snapped him out of his thoughts. "Yoooo," he answered.

"What you on, G?"

"Shit, coolin with Unc. What you on?"

"I need to holla at you face to face its important too, gang."

"Aight, where at?" Blake asked and Blue sent him a location to meet him at. He also told him to bring a homie. Blake rushed out of his home and rode to the Hundreds to pick up Wet Em Up and they met Blue on 97th and Merrill. Blake climbed out of his Benz and hopped to Blake's car.

"Aye, do you know a King named RaRa?" he asked after climbing in Blake's backseat.

"Naw, who is he?" Blake asked, looking at Blue through the rearview mirror.

"I ain't never heard of him either, but my sister say he act like he's a somebody, she with him right now. "

"Where they at?"

"At one of his cribs on 97th Street. I told her to unlock the back door for us and keep him busy until we get there," Blue said, pulling out his Glock 19. Blake didn't like the idea of him sitting behind him with a gun in his hand, but he pulled off anyway. He texted Wet Em Up and told him to be on point, for all he knew this could be a set-up. Wet Em Up watched Blue like a hawk the whole ride. Once they got there, they rode through the block and a crowd of Latin Kings were posted outside.

"Damn we can't pop out right here, they gone be all over us," Blake said, riding past the crowd.

"We can leave the car on the next block and come through the alley," Blue suggested.

Blake didn't like the sound of that at all. This nigga Blue was tryna get him in an alley on the Latin Kings' block. He could easily lead him back there, have him killed and blame it on the Kings and nobody would question it.

"Wet, you can drop me and Blue off in the alley and when I call you, pull up in front of the crib and handle the crowd for us while we get up outta that bitch," Blake said. If it was a trap, he didn't want to lead Wet Em Up in it with him, this wasn't his beef at all. They pulled in the alley and Blake and Blue hopped out. They walked down the alley until they were in the backyard of the house Millie was in.

The whole walk down the alley was creepy to Blake, his eyes darted in every direction looking for any signs of danger. When they made it, they saw the only way in the backyard was to climb over a big wooden fence. Blake jumped up to look over the fence to make sure it wasn't any dogs or humans waiting for them. He thought about letting Blue go over first, but he didn't want to catch a headshot coming down off the fence, so he quickly flipped over.

Once at the back door, Blake twisted the knob and the door came open. He nodded for Blue to go first. He felt more comfortable in the back. They crept through the clean, plush home with guns aimed and ready. Blake's heart pounded in his chest as he moved through the house. On the second floor of the home, they heard Trey Songz playing softly in the room closest to the stairwell. They tiptoed to the door and Blue swung it open to see Millie bent over the bed with her big ass tooted while sucking RaRa's dick.

"Get the fuck up, Millie!" he growled. RaRa reached for the .40 he had sitting on his nightstand, but Millie had already discreetly knocked it on the floor out of his reach.

"You said keep him busy," Millie blushed, putting on her jeans. She caught Blake watching her jump into her pants and dropped her eyes to the floor. RaRa tried to jump out of the bed, but a shot from Blue's Glock knocked him back down. Blake ran up and pumped three shots into RaRa's chest before grabbing the iPhone that sat on his nightstand. He put RaRa's thumb on it to unlock it and scrolled through his contacts. He found Ice's name and *FaceTimed* him. Before Ice answered, he flipped the camera to RaRa's lifeless body.

"What's up, brother?" Ice answered, not paying attention to the camera.

"Look at me, bitch!" Blake said. Once Ice looked at the camera his face dropped. "Ahh-haa!" Blake teased before flipping the camera to his face. He knew he was being careless, but Ice rubbed it in every time he fucked one of his people up, so he was just returning the favor. "And we bout to kill everybody that's outside. Stop hidin', you scary ass Paisa," Blake told him before hanging up and calling Wet Em Up off his phone.

Wet Em Up pulled up in front of RaRa's crib and hopped out blowing his Glock 27 at the crowd of Latin Kings. Blake, Blue and Millie shot out of the house. Millie ran straight to Blake's car, but Blake and Blue joined the fire fight. A couple of the Kings shot back, but they were caught off guard, so the others who were carrying guns were in the "run first, shoot later" mind state. When their clips were empty, Blake and Blue jetted to the car and Wet Em Up reversed up the block, going in the opposite direction as the Kings.

***

After dropping Blue and Millie off to their cars, Blake and Wet Em Up stopped at the gas station on 83rd and State. Wet Em Up was about to hop and go grab some woods but Blake stopped him. "Hold on, there go a few of the guys that's been actin like it's smoke with me," he said, pointing at a gray Chevy Impala. Lil Moe and a fewof his homies were in the car.

"So, what you tryna do?" Wet Em Up asked. All Blake had to do was give him the word and he would turn the gas station into a horror scene.

"I'm bout to follow they ass and when we get the chance you know what time it is," Blake said. After a few minutes, the Impala pulled out of the lot. He waited a few seconds before pulling out behind them. He made sure he stayed at least two cars behind them. The Impala pulled into the churches chicken parking lot on 79th and pulled next to a Black Benz. "Ooohhhh, that's KD hoe ass!" Blake said excitedly, pointing towards the Benz. He maneuvered his car into the lot and Wet Em Up hopped out shooting. KD's Benz screeched off like a bat out of hell.

The car Lil Moe was in was in neutral, so it wasn't as quick to move. Whoever was driving put the car in reverse and tried to back away from the shots. Blake jumped out and ran up on the Impala, throwing in the windshield. Once his gun clicked empty, he turned around and bolted back to his car. The Impala got smacked by a Hyundai on its way out of the lot, causing a big collision. Blake knew for a fact that he had scored, it was no way everyone who was in the Impala made it out unscathed.

Chapter 8

Cordale entered the basement of the abandoned house to see that Ladale was woke, seemingly waiting on him. The heavy, dark bags under Ladale's eyes were more from stress than lack of sleep. Telling his story was taking a toll on him. With every revelation he revealed, he was able to see the pain his brother was feeling. It was like he was the one with the gun, and Cordale was the one tied to the chair getting tortured by his words. Cordale took a seat on the crates he'd left sitting in front of Ladale, pulled out a Newport and lit it up. "I'm listening," he said blowing a cloud of smoke in Ladale's face.

Summer 1997

"Do he fuck you like I do?" Ladale asked his freak while pounding her out from behind. She had tried to move on with her life, but he had a spell on her that always made her find her way back to him.

"No," his freak moaned.

"When do you plan on telling him the truth?"

"I don't know it's not that easy," she replied. Her pussy was so wet that Ladale lost his train of thought for a moment and couldn't remember what he wanted to say so he focused on the task at hand. When he felt her body tremble and a curse word slipped through her juicy lips, he knew she had a orgasm so he pulled out and started eating her pussy from behind. He knew exactly how she liked it. He was a master when it came to pleasing her. After making her cum with his tongue, he got back behind her and fucked her like a madman until he came.

"So, you love that nigga more than you love me?" he asked after a couple of minutes of them cuddling.

"That shouldn't even be a question, Ladale."

"I'm only asking because that's how you been making me feel lately," he replied with a hint of sadness in his tone. He was a master manipulator. He knew exactly how to play on her feelings and get her to bend at his will.

"What have I been doing to make you feel like that?"

"You give that lame ass nigga all your time. From the outside looking in, you look happy as hell playing house with him. That shit hurting me in ways I can't even explain."

"This was all a part of your plan. You started this sick game and now you mad at me for doing exactly what you told me to do."

"So, you still mine?"

"Of course," the freak said, giving Ladale a peck on the lips. "And to show you that I'm still yours, I'ma get him out of the house tonight, so you can get in and clear it out."

"That's my baby," Ladale smiled, giving her a passionate kiss. They laid there, plotting on hitting the home she shared with her boyfriend. He was always able to convince her to steal money or drugs from him whenever he needed it. He knew he had full mind control over her, but in all actuality, he was insecure because he knew he couldn't compete with her man, and he wasn't blind to the fact that he was starting to lose control. Before he lost it completely, he would milk her dry.

Later that night, Ladale sat in Cordale's kitchen with the gang and a few women. The guys were playing spades for a hundred a game, it was him and Cordale, against Willis and Winky. Ladale was trying to focus on the card game, but he couldn't stop stealing glances at TayTay, every so often he caught her looking too.

"Let's go out tonight, baby. I wanna do something fun," TayTay told Cordale.

"Like what?" Cordale asked, after slamming the queen of spade on the table and scooping up the book he just won.

Let's go bowling or skating."

"Y'all fuckin with it?" he asked the guys.

"Naw, I don't feel like bussin my ass in front of a hundred people tonight," Willis said, speaking up before anyone else.

"Well, let's go bowling if you don't want to skate," Willis' baby mother Sade chimed in. He really didn't want to do anything besides hustle, go in the house and watch a good movie. He felt like having too much fun distracted him from stacking his paper, but on the other hand, he did whatever to make Sade smile. So, if she wanted to go out and have a good time her wish was his command.

"A'ight, let's play a few more hands right here, so I can win all of Ladale's money. He probably ain't got too much left anyway," he quipped snidely.

"You don't even play that good," Ladale scoffed. He wanted to take a shot at Willis' pockets, but he knew he couldn't talk money with him. Willis was on a whole 'nother level financially.

"Let's put five hundred on this game," Willis said. Ladale was so consumed in watching TayTay's ass as she left the room, he spoke without realizing what he was saying. "Bet," he said quickly.

"Five hundred gone hurt you, boy," Willis cracked, making Ed and Winky laugh.

"Whatever, nigga," Ladale mumbled, standing up. "I gotta piss before we start," he said rushing off to the upstairs master bathroom. TayTay was in the bathroom looking in the mirror, when he entered and came up behind her. He wrapped his arms around her waist, while planting soft kisses on the nape of her neck.

"Stop it," she whispered, snatching away from him.

"Why?" Ladale asked. Ever since they'd had sex, he had fallen head over heels in love with her. He had caught her on another drunk night, and she had asked him to eat her pussy. He did and they ended up having sex afterwards. He was under the impression she was starting to catch feelings for him. His feelings for her were as real as they got, so her sudden rejection stung a bit.

"Because we can't do this." She shook her head. "We should've never done anything in the first place. Your brother loves me, and I can't disrespect him any longer."

Ladale's face twisted into a mixed mask of frustration and anger. "Stop playin and let me get a kiss or something!" he said, stepping in her face.

"No!" she said, forcefully shoving him away. "I made a mistake by doing anything with you."

"So, what if I go tell him? Do you think he still gone love you?" Ladale asked bitterly. He couldn't hide the fact that he was salty, in fact he was so salty, he really was ready to go and tell Cordale about their little fiasco and ruin everything they had.

"You can't do that, Ladale. Please don't do that," TayTay pleaded.

"Why shouldn't I?"

"Because I'm pregnant," TayTay said, and his face dropped. All she could see in his eyes was hurt and deep beyond that hurt, she could see a glimmer of hope.

"By who?" he asked.

"Cordale," TayTay replied, breaking his heart into a billion pieces.

"It could be mines, doe. We never used protection."

"I know for a fact it's his."

"How?" Ladale asked and she couldn't answer. He was about to say something, but Willis called him to come play cards. "We gone talk," he told TayTay before rushing out of the bathroom.

***

January 1998

Ladale stood next to TayTay's bed in the delivery room at Little Mother of Mary's Hospital. She was going into labor, preparing to deliver her son. Cordale and Willis were waiting in the waiting room, because Cordale had a weak stomach and couldn't watch her give birth. "Do you think we could take a blood test?" Ladale asked her. He had spent her whole nine months of pregnancy trying to convince her it was a big possibility the baby she was carrying was his. He had added up the dates from the times they had sex, until her expected due date. The dates added up and that was something that scared her. She prayed the baby wasn't his, that would ruin her whole life.

"No Ladale, just leave it alone!" she snapped.

"And why should I just leave it alone?"

"Because your brother loves me and I love him too, we're happy together. Why would you want to ruin our happiness?"

"If that's my child, I deserve the right to be in his life."

"And you still can be, just as his uncle," TayTay said, crushing Ladale. He turned away so she couldn't see the hurt in his expression. "You already got a son out here that you don't even claim," TayTay said, causing him to turn back around.

"What?" he asked, raising an eyebrow.

"You thought I didn't know that you was fucking Sade?"

"Who told you that?"

"She did and she told me Willis' son Meechie is really your son and it's a possibility the little girl she just had could be yours too."

Ladale stood there looking stupid, he thought nobody knew about him and Sade. He kept their relationship hidden. She was his little freak. "What else did she tell you?"

"All the bogus shit you had her doing to Willis—" TayTay was saying until a contraction sent a sharp pain ripping through her body.

Ladale stood by TayTay's bedside during her whole delivery. When the pain became too much for her to bare, it was his hand she held on to and squeezed until it felt like it was going numb. He used a wet towel to wipe sweat off her forehead, and when the baby was on his way out, it was him urging for her to push. He was doing everything a father should've been doing. TayTay wanted to name her son Cordale Jr., they would've called him CJ. But she told Ladale if he promised to keep their secret, she would name her son after their father to honor both him and Cordale. Ladale agreed and that's where Lil Ced got his name from.

When he came out, the nurses wiped him off and his dark brown eyes mesmerized Ladale, he knew without a doubt Lil Ced was his seed. He cradled the wailing baby in his arms for a second. He hated that he couldn't be with TayTay and raise Lil Ced with her as a family. He looked at her and hatred filled his heart. He passed Lil Ced to her and stood in the corner of the room while the nurse fetched Cordale and Willis.

***

Present Day

Cordale shook his head from left to right, he had an enormous lump in his throat and his heart felt like a volcano that was on the verge of erupting. If it did erupt, then pain from betrayal would spew out like molten lava, consuming anything he touched with its intensity. He couldn't believe what his brother had just told him. He couldn't believe TayTay betrayed his trust and love like that. A lone tear escaped the corner of his eye, he didn't try to catch it he could only hope to contain the ocean that hid behind his eyes.

"I always wanted to tell you, bruh, I just didn't know how," Ladale said sadly. He knew he was living on borrowed time. It was no way that Cordale was letting him walk out of that basement, so he had no reason to lie. He had no more energy to manipulate.

"Fuck all that story shit, fuck digging up the past, why did you kill her?" Cordale asked. He didn't want to find anything else out, if he didn't know it already, he was ok with not knowing it. The only thing he wanted now was the closure he came for.

"Because she got tired of me blackmailing her. How do you think I was getting the information to hijack your loads?" Ladale asked. When Cordale took too long to respond, he continued, "She would be right there whenever y'all chose a destination and a route and she would let me know, that was part of our agreement. If I kept you in the dark about our past, then she would help me rob you when she could. She only agreed to that after I threatened to expose her.

"I know it sounds fucked up, but she really hated doing that shit. She loved you deeply and would've done anything to protect your feelings. I started growing hatred and resentment for you and her the moment Lil Ced was born. It was like when he was born, I died. I feel like you stole God's gift to me. Over the years, that hatred and pain grew into something uncontrollable. TayTay was done and instead of letting her walk away, I killed her," Ladale explained.

Cordale got up and punched him so hard that he almost lost consciousness, he followed up with another punch that rattled his jaw and almost knocked his chair over. "I did everything for you, bruh!" he growled, connecting powerful punch after powerful punch. "You ain't deserve shit, but I made sure you had it all!"

"I know, bruh, I'm sorry. I loved her—" Ladale was saying through swollen, bloody lips but was silenced by a couple more punches. Cordale couldn't stop swinging, his rage was in control, and he let it drive. When Ladale's chair toppled over, he straddled him and started beating his face in. He thought about TayTay and Lil Ced. He thought about Meechie and Shana. He thought about the war with Willis.

With every thought came more hatred for his brother. They were all innocent and had lost their lives behind the wicked game he was playing. He was to blame for all the pain that Cordale had endured. Fuck shooting Ladale, he felt like that was too easy a death for someone as evil as him, he wanted to beat him to death. He deserved to have his face mashed in by the person for who he had caused the most pain, who ironically was the person who had shown him the most love.

Cordale punched Ladale savagely, the scrapes and cuts on his hands were supposed to hurt but they felt good to him. Somehow during the beating, the chair broke and the ropes around Ladale's hands loosened, and he was able to pull them free. Cordale was caught completely off guard when Ladale snatched the Glock off his waist. Ladale lifted the gun, which felt extremely heavy to him, and tried to shoot Cordale in his chin but missed. Cordale grabbed the gun by the barrel, and they began to wrestle over it.

Ladale truly felt bad for the wrongs he'd done to his brother, but not so bad that he would just lay there and die without a fight. If it was him or Cordale, he would pick himself every time. Fuck Cordale. He squeezed the trigger again, this time a bullet skinned Cordale's neck. Cordale let out an animalistic roar before headbutting Ladale, breaking his nose on impact. He headbutted him again for good measure and Ladale's grip on the gun loosened. Cordale quickly snatched the gun out of his hand, pressed the barrel against his forehead and pulled the trigger. One shot burst Ladale's head open, splashing Cordale with his thoughts and brain matter.

The warm blood on his skin felt good to Cordale. The sight of Ladale's open skull looked like a priceless painting to him.

He pumped three more shots into Ladale's head and then ten more in his chest. Ladale was the devil, a monster, and he had to make sure he killed the monster so he couldn't return.

Cordale sat on Ladale's lifeless body for a few seconds before standing up. When he got up, he popped the clip out of his Glock to see he had two bullets left. For maybe the millionth time since losing TayTay, he contemplated suicide. With all the hurt he was feeling, death seemed like the peace he deserved. Only a small piece of him felt revitalized, like Ladale's death had lifted all the weight of the world from his shoulders. And now, he felt so light he felt he could get lifted off his feet by a small gust of wind.

The gun felt so good in his hand, like it belonged there. One pull of the trigger could cease the pain he was feeling. Once again, he couldn't find either the strength or the cowardice to pull the trigger. He was either too strong or too weak to kill himself. He took one last look at Ladale before tucking his gun and leaving the house.

Inside the car, Cordale drove for a few blocks until he was comfortably away from the house and pulled over. He sent a text to Blake, asking for Blue's number. Once he had Blue's number he texted him, asking for another number. In the sixty seconds it took for Blue to respond, Cordale felt himself start to unravel. When the number came back, he stared at it for a couple minutes, wondering the best way to ask what he needed to ask. It was really no wrong or right way to ask any of the questions that he needed answered. His nerves were getting the best of him and before he talked himself out of making the call, he tapped the screen and initiated the call.

"Hello?" a woman answered after a few rings.

"Sade?" Cordale asked. His heart was beating so loudly he wondered if she could hear it from the other end of the phone.

"Yes, may I ask who this is?"

"Cordale," he replied, and the line went quiet. For a second, he thought she had hung up on him until she spoke.

"Hey, Cordale, what's going on?" Sade asked, she hadn't heard from him in over a decade and was surprised by his call.

"It's a lot going on," he said, shaking his head as if she could see him. "And I need your help straightening this shit out."

"What's up?" Sade asked, her stomach was doing flips. The way he was sounding scared her, she immediately started thinking that something happened with Willis. But then again, she had just spoken to him thirty minutes ago, so she quickly dismissed that thought.

"I need to ask you something, and I need for you to be completely honest with your answer."

"Oh... okay," she replied slowly.

"Before Ladale died—"

"Ladale's dead?" Sade asked, cutting Cordale off. The twinge of hurt he heard in her voice was unmistakable.

"Yeah, and before he died, we had a brother-to-brother conversation in an attempt to reconcile and he put everything on the table. He told me about you and him, he told me Meechie was really his son, and it was a possibility Shana was his too, was any of that the truth?"

"I had to do what was best for me and my son," Sade said, defending her actions. He could hear the emotion in her voice. "Ladale wasn't capable of being the father Willis was, Willis took care of me, he bettered me and made sure me and our children had the best. Ladale wouldn't have been able to do that. He was selfish, it was all about him. Not only that, but if Willis had known Meechie was Ladale's son and not his, he would've went crazy. The war between y'all would've been started," Sade said. As much as Cordale hated to admit it, she was absolutely right, she had a valid point. Things would've been different, but they probably would've still ended the same, a bunch of innocents dying behind a war they had nothing to do with.

"Lil Ced and Shana were in love. Did you ever think about the fact they could've been related?"

"Yes!" Sade snapped. She was crying now. She never imagined this part of her past would ever be brought into the light. "My daughter loved Lil Ced more than she loved anybody else or anything. The worst times of her life was when she couldn't be with him. She hated her father because she felt like he was forcing her to live, without the one person she couldn't live without. She was happy with Lil Ced and what kind of mother would I have been, if I would've crushed that love? Please don't try to make me out as a bad person for my decision to put my children first. That's a mother's duty and if I could go back, I would do it all over again the exact same way,"

"I'm not trying to make you feel bad because I completely understand why you did what you did. I understand your logic, I just wish things could've been different," Cordale said before breaking down. The floodgates broke and an ocean of tears paraded down his face. "I miss them so much," he cried.

"I miss them too," Sade said. For the next ten minutes they sat on the phone listening to each other cry, sniffle and sob. Neither said a word, they communicated through sorrow and they both understood each other completely. "So, now what?" she asked.

"I don't know," Cordale replied with a shrug. "I won't tell anyone about this conversation, it's not my business and the damage is done. Digging in the past will only hurt everyone involved. Ladale is gone and all the chaos he created and the bullshit he was wrapped up in, should die with him. I just needed for you to confirm his story. Thank you for being honest with me."

"No problem, Cordale," Sade replied softly, and they sat on the line for a few more minutes. Neither knew what to say and neither truly wanted to end the call.

"Cordale," she said.

"Yeah, I'm here."

"Enjoy whatever time you got left. Life's been so hard to us that I believe that you deserve to be happy. Please find you some peace and enjoy it," she said.

"I will, Sade, and you make sure you do the same," Cordale said, before hanging up the phone.

Chapter 9

KD pulled up on the block, jumped out his car with his Glock in his hand, and scurried into the crib where Lil Moe was waiting for him. Once inside, he put his Glock on his waist and locked the door. Lil Moe, along with a few other guys, were sitting in the living room of the home, shaking and bagging up heroin.

"What's the word, Gang?" KD asked Lil Moe, dropping a gang sign with him before taking a seat across from him at the table.

"Shit, we had ran out, so I had bro nem shake up that fifty grams you gave me earlier. They been eating this shit up."

"That's that Fentanyl."

"Keep that shit comin then," Lil Moe replied. "Aye, on Lil Ced grave, that was Blake hoe ass that blew us down at Church's."

"How you know?"

"I saw his tall, yellow ass. He the one that ran up on our shit," Lil Moe said.

Blake had killed two of the guys that night.

"You sure?"

"On Lil Ced," Lil Moe repeated, and KD pulled out his phone.

Thirty minutes later, they were parked in front of a crib on 106th and Indiana. He called Von D and seconds later, Von was on the porch waving them over. They got out and followed him inside the crib, where a few of his homies were playing *NBA2K* on a large flatscreen that hung off the wall.

"What y'all on?" Von D asked, shaking up with both of them before grabbing a pound of Cheetah Piss and fishing out a few chunks. He then pulled out a pack of Backwoods and began unraveling one.

"Shit, I came to holla at you about that nigga Blake," KD replied.

"What happened?"

"That nigga killed two of the guys the other night,"

"No, he didn't!" Von D said in disbelief.

"On Lil Ced, he did. He caught us at Church's on 79th and fucked us up," Lil Moe said.

Nobody peeped it but Wet Em Up, who was sitting on the couch bussing Boothie's ass in *2K*, stiffened up when the two guys mentioned the shooting at Church's. He wondered if they knew he was with Blake, and they were there to get down on him.

Von D shook his head at first when KD was in his ear about how much of a snake Blake was. He didn't pay it much mind because he didn't see it. Blake welcomed him with open arms, he showed him love from day one and helped him run his bag up, so he never saw any snake in him up until recently. He'd heard about him claiming that he "accidently" killed Knuckles, and how he smoked Man trying to smoke KD. Not to mention how he started fucking Aisha while she was in a relationship with KD. All that, on top of how he left Lil Hot on a hit, had Von D starting to feel like maybe KD was on to something.

"I'm not gone lie to you, gang. On Lil Ced, I feel like we need to get that nigga out the way before he dunk one of us," KD said, grabbing the smoldering Backwood that Von was trying to hand him and taking a few hits of the potent weed.

"I don't think that's the move right there."

"How come it ain't?" KD asked with a frown. "That nigga ain't giving nobody no passes, so why should we?"

"Y'all got something personal going on over Aisha, and I can't condone y'all killing each other over some pussy, that's lame shit. On Stone."

"On Lil Ced this not over no pussy," KD lied quickly. "We heard he be out here through y'all shit a lot. You can just have one of yo homies call us whenever he slide through, or one of them can clap his ass and collect that bread King nem got on him," KD said.

Von D smacked his lips, KD was right there frontin his shit sounding just as much a snake as he was tryna make Blake seem. *Birds of a feather flock together*, Von thought. "Hell naw, that shit dead. On Stone! If y'all gone kill each other, then y'all gone do that shit on y'all own time. We ain't comin like that out here," he told KD with a mug. "And you wild as hell for saying another mufucka can cash bro in, that's some weird shit."

"On Lil Ced, that's not weird shit, him tryna back door everybody, that's what's weird. Just stay away from his ass and tell yo peoples to do the same, cause we not sparing nobody when it's time to get him."

"What that mean?" Von D asked, not missing the threat in KD's last statement. Wet Em Up and Boothie had paused their game and was fully focused on the conversation they were having. Boothie was a little lost, but Wet Em Up was on point, ready to get active.

"We on that nigga ass and it's up there on sight with him, we don't want none of y'all getting caught up in that crossfire," Lil Moe said in an attempt to clear up what KD had said.

"Look," Von D said, running a hand over his face. "Like I said before, we don't got shit to do with what y'all got going on. I fuck with Blake just like I fuck with y'all. On Black P Stone, if you send a shot at me or one of mines, or even if you let off a shot on my block, it's gone be whatever it's gone be," he said in a calm tone. Behind the tone was a clear message. *Keep that shit between y'all, or else*.

KD held Von's gaze for a few seconds before chuckling. "Say less," he said, standing up. "Let me get some of that Gas," he said after stretching his chunky body.

"Take the pound," Von D told him.

"We bout to get in traffic, hit my line later, gang," KD told him before dropping a gang sign with him and leaving.

Von D wanted to call Blake and let him know how KD was coming but he decided maybe it was best if he minded his business. He was loyal to both of them and refused to pick a side.

"Them niggas tweakin," Wet Em Up said to Von D, who was now rolling up a wood stuffed with Birthday Cake. "I fuck with Blake hard. I feel like they was lowkey talking about me."

"Knowing yo hot ass, you probably been with him puttin that belt on they ass."

"Hell naw," Wet Em Up lied with a chuckle. "I only fucked up the Kings with him a few times."

"Good keep it that way. Them niggas tweaking over a bitch, you know we not moving like that at all. We got this bitch rolling, we bout to run our bag up. That's it, that's all."

"How much Blake got on his head?" Boothie asked still thinking about what KD had just said. If the price was right, he would most definitely dunk his ass, he didn't fuck with him like that.

"Some slight shit," Von D replied, not wanting to talk about it. "I know somebody who got a Hellcat Charger for sale and they got the title to it," he said, changing the subject.

"How much they want for it?" Boothie asked. While he and Von discussed the price, Wet Em Up got up from the couch, went to the front porch and called Blake to let him know everything that had just been said.

***

Mo Money, Bang and Domo were riding through the Hundreds, looking for Blake's Maserati. They had gotten a call from Chito saying that he had a girlfriend from Risky Road. That was where Mo Money was from, and he was curious as to who Blake was fucking from his block. He asked Chito for the woman's name, but he didn't know it. Bang was irate that they hadn't killed any of the three men they were after. This was unlike them. KD was most likely the first one who would get caught, because he was always out and about. He was always in his hood, but he stayed on point, so it wasn't an easy task getting up on him. He was very cautious and aware of his
surroundings so every time they made a move on him, it ended in a blick out.

Blake was more elusive than KD was, he didn't play his hood at all and up until now, they didn't know where else to look for him. He had deactivated all of his social media and he stayed away from the camera, so it was hard to really get the drop on him.

Von D proved to be the hardest challenge due to the fact that they couldn't dig up anything about him. Nobody had ever heard of a Von from Evans Mob or Eight Trey Mob. It was like he was a ghost. Mo Money was the only one who knew that the Von they were looking for was actually his homie Von from D Block. He kept Bang in the dark, in hopes to protect his friend. He was trying to figure out which one of them was working with the Kings. Whoever it was, he was trying hard to *oop* his boys and pop out when the smoke clears, typical hoe nigga shit. Mo Money wanted to find out who it was so he could smash him first or at least before he got Von hurt.

"There go a Maserati turning up Indiana," Bang told Mo Money, pointing towards the car, which was almost out of sight. They were a few blocks away, passing King Drive. Mo Money was driving, and he did everything he could to catch up with the car without being too noticeable. Once he turned on Indiana, he couldn't see the Maserati driving anymore. He rode slowly down Indiana, making sure he paid attention to his surroundings. Once he passed 105th and Indiana, he was entering D Block's territory.

D Block was once Mo Money's second home, He did everything on those blocks, lost a lot of blood, sweat and tears for that block. But just like his first home, Risky Road, he wasn't anymore welcomed on D Block. If the wrong person caught him cruising through the hood, they would try to kill him, or if he so happened to see the wrong person, let's just say some of the best things in life came free.

"There go the Masi right there," Bang said, "he must be in one of these cribs." Mo Money hit the block and sat a few cars behind the Maserati they were assuming was Blake's. His eyes darted from one cut to another, remembering every gangway they used to get from Prairie to Indiana, and from Indiana to Edbrooke. He knew those cuts like the back of his hand. He was also trying to watch every crib. He could see where his homie Trell and Von D used to live, the crib his cousin Nutso grew up in, and a few of their old freaks' old homes. Being on Indiana brought back memories, some good, some bad. He tried shaking them out of his head, but he couldn't.

"Look at Tony Moon baldhead ass." He smiled watching a short, bald dark-skinned guy with a full beard, walking with a hype no doubt he was still out there serving.

"Who is that?" Bang asked KD, gripping his Micro Draco, he was itching to pop out and fuck somebody up. It'd been a while since he fucked somebody over and like a vampire, he needed blood.

"One of the big bros from the hood, he good, he ain't on shit," Mo Money replied already knowing what he was on. A couple of shorties walking up Indiana caught their attention. Well, they caught Mo Money and Bang's attention. Domo was in the backseat nodding off the Perc, with a big ass Glock 21 sitting on his lap. The shorties didn't look like the gang-banging type, they didn't look grimy and rough like Mo Money and his crowd did at fourteen-fifteen years old. They looked like all they wanted to do was play *2K* or *Grand Theft Auto* online, instead of gangbanging and hitting licks, but nowadays looks could be very deceiving. A nigga could look soft as hell but have three or four bodies. The shorties walked past their car oblivious to the danger that lurked behind the tinted windows. They weren't even on point, so Mo Money knew they weren't a threat.

The way they were just walking and joking, without looking out for police or opps let them know they weren't carrying a weapon, they would most likely be victims of stray bullets. That was the sad reality of having to grow up in Chicago.

"Look," Bang said, nudging Mo Money, snapping him out of his thoughts. "There go Blake on that porch," he said, unlocking his door. "Domo!" he said, waking his cousin up.

Mo Money looked at the porch where four people were standing, three guys and one bitch. Blake was instantly recognizable, because he was over six feet, with extremely light skin. The nigga standing next to Blake was looking towards 107th Street and then towards 105th, that's when Mo Money was able to get a full glimpse of his face. "Hold on!" he told Bang, who was about to hop out and run up on the porch with his Draco.

"Fuck you mean wait?" he snarled with a mug on his face.

"The nigga he with, that's my peoples."

"Man, dude got half a million on his head. Yo peoples a understand that."

"Naw," Mo Money said, shaking his head while watching Blake and Von D talk and laugh like they were the best of friends. "Not right now, not while he with my shorty," he said, before pulling out of the spot he was in.

"On BPSN, you tweakin!" Bang snapped. Denying him the chance to kill was like denying a man in the desert an ice-cold Sprite. It was a sin and it pissed him off, he was madder about not being able to kill Blake, than not being able to collect the bounty.

As they rode past the porch, Von D, Blake and their homie watched the car, trying to see who was in it or if it was a threat. They all had their hands near their guns, just in case it went down.

"That's that bitch!" Domo shouted from the backseat. "Stop! Pull over! That's that bitch!" he said, trying to open his door. He thought his mind was playing tricks on him when he first glanced at the dark-skinned woman who was standing next to Blake. The Perc had him drowsy but as they rode past, he was able to see her eyes. He knew he wasn't tweaking, Aisha, his bitch, was standing right there.

"Where, cuz?" Bang asked.

"On the porch with them niggas! Stop the mufuckin car, you goofy ass nigga!" he yelled at Mo Money, who was now making a right off Indiana, headed towards Michigan.

"I just told you we wasn't standing on shit while my homie was on location," Mo Money replied firmly. He was doing a good job at holding his composure. The way Domo was talking to him was the reason many niggas were dead, out of respect for Bang, he was trying to be cool.

"Come on, mane, that's the bitch that stole all that money and drugs from me. I need to snatch that bitch up!" Domo said frantically.

"At least pull back around so we can lamp on em," Bang suggested.

Mo Money shook his head. "If we go back around, they gone be on the car, didn't you see how they was on us when we rode past?" he asked, driving down Michigan towards 103rd. He peeked at Domo through the rearview mirror, he was breathing heavy, mean mugging him while clutching his gun. "What?" Mo Money asked him, flashing a mug of his own.

"Bruh, stop talking to me 'fore I smo—"

"Leave that shit alone, cuz," Bang said, cutting Domo off, he knew that he was about to make a threat and he knew Mo Money didn't take threats kindly. Bang was just as angry as Domo was but he knew that there was always a method to Mo Money's madness. "Now we know shorty either be with Blake, or she be on Indiana. Either way we finally found her ass," Bang said, trying to make it make sense.

"Fuck all that shit, cuz. We could've just clapped Blake and snatched Aisha up if we wasn't with this goofy, scary ass nigga!" Domo snapped. What he knew that the rest of the car didn't, was that he only had so long to be back in Memphis with the drugs and money that she stole, before the men he was doing business with greenlighted a hit on him. He was locked in with some Nigerian Vice Lords who were connected in the medical underworld, and they flooded him and his father with any pharmaceutical drug they thought they could move. They had a good thing going until Aisha ruined it and now she had Domo in the hotseat.

Mo Money chuckled while watching Domo through the rearview mirror, he was on the verge of talking himself into a slot at the cemetery. Mo Money occasionally took peeps over at Bang, tryna gauge his stance in it all. He felt like it was two against one, even though Bang hadn't said anything. Domo was his cousin, and they were both acting mad so he was going off that energy. Mo Money pulled into a gas station right off the E-way on 79th. "I'm bout to go grab some woods and shit. One of y'all hop in the driver's seat," he said, quickly jumping out the car.

He entered the gas station and stood at the counter while watching Domo climb out the back seat and into the driver's seat. Mo Money bought a pack of Backwoods, a fruit water, and a bag of peach rings before heading back to the car. He smiled while climbing into the backseat of the car, he was quick on his feet with his thinking. "Aye Bang, how about you drive? You know he don't know the city like you do, just in case we gotta go on a high speed," he suggested.

Domo smacked his lips, but it made sense, so he and Bang switched seats. This was all a part of Mo Money's plan. He wanted to be in the back behind both of them and since he felt like Bang was the bigger threat, he put him in the driver's seat so he would have to drive and watch his mirrors, therefore limiting his ability to watch him. Mo Money ate his peach rings in silence for a while, while Bang navigated through the city.

"Aye, what was to that goofy, scary shit you was just talkin bout?" Mo Money said to Domo, leaning forward behind him, pressing the barrel of his Glock 31 to the side of his neck.

"What?" Domo asked, caught off guard. Mo Money noticed a little of that aggressiveness had vanished from his tone. Mo Money quickly reached up and snatched his Glock off his lap.

"Stop playin, Money," Bang said, not even looking over. If he had he would've been able to see that Mo Money was dead serious. In the back of his mind, he knew it, he just thought he had stopped it before it got too far.

"You was just sitting behind me huffin and puffin, clutching yo pipe like you was ready to do something. Where that energy at now?" Mo Money asked.

"Bruh, get that gun off of me," Domo said calmly. That got Bang's attention.

"Money what the fuck is you doing, Law? You got a gun to his neck like he not my cousin?" Bang barked, looking over.

"I know he yo cousin and that's why I'ma need for you to keep both hands on the wheel," Mo Money replied. "I don't know who you thought I was, but I'm not him. You not gone handle me any way, and you gone watch what come out yo mouth when you talking to me. Niggas get killed behind name calling," he told Domo before turning back to Bang. "Pull in the alley," he told him.

"Don't do that, Moe," Bang warned, he knew exactly what was on his homie's mind.

"Man pull in the alley," Mo Money replied sharply. Bang pulled in the alley, thinking he was about to cross the line and kill his blood. Instead of killing Domo like he wanted to, Mo Money hopped out the car and took off through a gangway, he left Domo's gun laying on the backseat.

***

Later that night, Mo Money was sitting in a Jeep Compass on 106th and Indiana. He had to holla at Von D. He was watching the crib Von D nem had come out of earlier that day. At around 12:45 am, two dread heads left out the house and stood on the front porch. Both had long dreads, but the one with the longest dreads stood there watching the other one leave. Mo Money knew they were hustling out of the crib, because it had been nonstop traffic up until about an hour ago.

As soon as the guy in the car pulled off and his homie re-entered the crib, Mo Money got out his Jeep, ran up the stairs and knocked on the door. Boothie swung the door open to see Mo Money standing there with his Glock aimed. "Call Von," Mo Money told him, pushing him back into the crib. Twenty minutes later, Von D was entering the trap with a mug on his face. As soon as he entered the living room, his expression went from mad to shocked, to a slight grin when he saw Mo Money, sitting next to Boothie on the couch, with his gun aimed at his ribs.

"Mo Money, you gotta slow down man." He chuckled, closing the space between them. Mo Money smiled before standing up to shake up with him. After they shook up, they embraced in a brotherly hug. "What's up, Law?" Von D asked.

"Shit broski, same shit as usual. You know how I'm comin," Mo Money said, taking a seat on the couch. When he had Boothie call Von D he had him tell him to pull up, it was an emergency, a life-or-death situation, and it could've been for him. He didn't want Boothie to say his name because he wasn't sure who Von might've been around. He trusted Von D, that's why he wanted to holla at him alone.

"What's going on that got you runnin in my spot?" Von D asked, taking a seat on the couch. He pulled out a thick pre-rolled wood and flamed it up.

"You got some paper on yo head, you and the nigga Blake who I saw you with earlier."

"When you see me with Blake?"

"We was on him earlier and he led us over here, we was waiting for him to come out and when he did, he was with you," Mo Money explained and Von D nodded.

"The Kings got money on you, him and some other nigga y'all be with named KD. Me and my homie been on y'all, but he think it's a Von from 79th or 83rd, the Kings think you from over there too."

"Yeah, I heard they got like two hundred fifty grand on us."

"It's half a million now," Mo Money stated, making both Von and Boothie's face drop. Boothie had to whistle at that number. "And the lil dark-skinned bitch, Iesha or something—"

"Aisha?"

"Yeah, her."

"That's my cousin, she fuckin with Blake."

"Damn," Mo Money said, shaking his head, the whole situation was getting more and more complicated. "Some nigga from Memphis up here and he looking for her, he saying she stole some money and drugs from him."

"I heard about that."

"Yeah, the nigga from Memphis… he out here with his cousin, who a real problem and they know about the bread the Kings got on y'all. That's who I was with earlier, it was us three. I stopped them earlier, but I won't be with them every time they out lurkin, so you gotta be careful," Mo Money warned. "And the Kings say they got somebody from y'all side working with them, so you gotta be careful around them niggas too."

"Damn man," was all Von could say before handing Mo Money the smoldering wood.

"I think you should just shoot O.T. you know,—*outta town*— for a while, until we get Blake and KD out the way and hopefully,

King nem will be satisfied with two out of three and just forget about you," Mo Money said, even though he knew that was unlikely.

"They probably won't forget shit."

"Why won't they?"

"Because I'm the one that killed Chito's brother," Von D confessed. Mo Money didn't say shit, but he didn't have to because his eyes said enough. Von was fucked.

"I'm saying doe, can you help me get Chito out the way?" Von D asked hopefully.

"It ain't impossible but it's close to it," Mo Money replied, crushing Von's hope. "But what I can do is help you stay alive until we can figure something out."

"Ain't shit I could do to get you to spare my peoples, huh?" Von asked.

Mo Money mulled it over for a minute. "I gotta check that mil off Blake and KD, plus they was gone hit my hand something decent for Aisha. But since she's your cousin and I don't like that hoe ass Memphis nigga, I can make sure she stay alive too, unless she get caught by them when I'm not around. The thing about that is they don't want her dead, they need her alive, so she can tell them where the drugs and money are. They want they shit back."

"You gotta be careful when you catch Blake doe, Gang,"

"Why?" Mo Money asked curiously.

"That's Jala's nigga, they been together for years now, she always in traffic with him or at his house, so you gotta make sure that she don't get caught up in the crossfire," Von said. He knew that adding Jala in the mix would affect Mo Money, she was his little cousin. He loved Jala to death, and she was his favorite.

"I thought Blake was fucking Aisha."

"He is, but Jala is his main, that's where his heart is."

"All well, I'll keep that in mind," Mo Money said, getting up preparing to leave. "Be safe out here, lil bro, keep yo eyes open and stay dangerous."

"You already know, Law," Von D replied as they shook up.

"I'ma be in touch," Mo Money said before leaving. He had a whole lot to think about and some tough decisions to make, hopefully whatever he decided to do ended up being the right thing. But sadly, one thing about the story of his life, nothing he did was the right thing.

Molotti

Chapter 10

Aisha used her tongue to trace the tattoos on Blake's chest while Muni Long sang softly through the Bluetooth speakers. 'When I met you, When I met you, I knew this was it, I never been in love like this. A love like ours, I prayed for it on my knees every night for some hours, and hours and hours," she sung expressing how Aisha truly felt for Blake. She had been in love before, but never like this. He wasn't perfect because nobody was, but she was absolutely sure he was perfect for her. She loved everything about him.

"You must be ready for another round," he said, grabbing her bare ass with his big hand. She loved how his touch felt. They had just gotten done with an intense, passionate sex session and the way she was kissing on his chest was starting to arouse him again.

"You know I'm not duckin no rec," Aisha shot back, grabbing his dick. She started kissing down his chest to his stomach and was on her way lower, when the ringing of his phone interrupted them.

"Yooo," Blake answered the *FaceTime* call from Blue.

"Aye Gang, I'm in this afterhours spot and yo boy KD and a few other niggas just walked in this bitch."

"Where at?" Blake asked, jumping out of bed, hurriedly getting dressed. Blue dropped his location. "I'm on my way," Blake told him before hanging up on him. He was so focused on getting dressed and making it out the house, he didn't notice the look of distress on Aisha's face. She understood that when money or the streets called, he had to answer, but he had to understand that she was still a woman and she had delicate feelings. Her heart was so fragile, he didn't have to drop it to hurt her. "I'll be right back, bae," Blake told her before rushing out without even giving her a kiss goodbye.

***

When Blake pulled up to the hole in the wall after hours spot, he called Blue. "I'm outside, Gang," he said, scanning the parking lot for familiar faces.

"Aight, these niggas acting like they on me," Blue replied looking across the room at KD and the niggas he was with, they were mugging him and had been watching him ever since they found out he was in the club.

"Aight, come outside. I'm in my Infiniti truck," Blake told him.

Minutes later, Blue was walking out the club, along with some tall, brown-skinned nigga. Seconds after they exited the club, KD was coming out, followed by a few of the folks. Blake had already gotten out of his truck and was ducked off behind a Nissan truck. He popped up shooting, waving his Glock 20 at KD and his crowd. The switch emptied the Glock in a second and Blake bolted towards his truck.

KD got knocked down by one of his homies trying to avoid a bullet, no matter how gangsta you thought you were, niggas panicked when they heard that switch going off. KD bounced up quickly and upped his Glock, movement out his peripheral caused him to look to his right, where he saw Blake hauling ass. KD started shooting, trying to take his head off. He saw Blake, Blue and some other dude all trying to climb into a black Infiniti truck.

As Blake climbed into the driver's seat of the truck, a bullet slammed into his leg, making him stumble and fall. He quickly recovered and slid into the truck. He ducked down and smashed his foot on the gas, peeling out the lot. KD jumped in his Benz, screeched out behind him and chased Blake down. Both drivers bobbed and weaved in and out of traffic. KD was able to get next to Blake's truck after Blake almost hit another car while running a red light. KD threw his arm out of his window and squeezed his trigger. The sound of his Glock screaming lit up the quiet night.

Blake's window shattered as KD emptied his clip and sped off. Blake felt that he had gotten shot again, first in his leg and now he felt that familiar burn in his arm. He pulled on a side block and ditched the gun he had before calling the paramedics. Everybody in the truck had gotten shot. Blue had gotten hit in his hand, and his homie got caught in his side and under his armpit.

They all seemed to be ok, until Blue's homie started struggling to breathe. They were rushed to Christ Hospital where Blue's homie died from his gunshot wounds.

***

Cordale and Von D rode through the city in Cordale's Lincoln Navigator, rotating a wood. Cordale had just gotten off the phone with KD, who was explaining what went down the night before at the after hours' spot. The way KD told his story made it seem like Blake was with Blue on some back door shit, and they killed his homie Buddah while trying to kill him, and that's when he chased them down. He kept bringing up the fact that Blue was from 47th Place and Blake was fucking with him, that was treason in its purest form.

"These lil niggas really tweakin," Cordale said, flaming up a Newport.

"Hell yeah, they is and all this shit really over Aisha." Cordale smacked his lips. His two best men were at odds over a woman. A woman always played some type of role in why a war was going on. Plenty of men lost their lives behind a woman. Plenty of men were doing life in jail over a woman. His son committed suicide over a woman. His brother betrayed him over a woman. To say he was disappointed in Blake and KD was an understatement.

"It's some nigga from Memphis that's out here looking for Aisha. He got some people behind him too, so we gotta keep her tucked," Von D said after exhaling a lungful of smoke and throwing the roach out the window.

"How you know that?"

Von D thought about revealing his conversation with Mo Money to Cordale, but he knew Mo Money was still on Blake and KD's asses and just in case he caught up with one of them, he didn't want it to seem like they were in cahoots and he ooped one of them. "A nigga I been dumpin pounds to told me that mufuckas were asking about a chick from out of town that was holding on the Percs and Xans," Von lied.

"What made him bring that shit to your attention?"

"Cause I was grabbing Percs from Blake, dumping them here and there, so dude asked me if I knew a chick that was holding. I asked why and that's when he told me that shit."

"So, who does the Memphis nigga supposed to have behind him?"

"Dude didn't know all that," Von replied quickly. "And I heard King nem upped the price to half a million and they claiming somebody from our side supposed to be working with them on some backdoor shit."

"Straight up?" Cordale asked Von, taking his eyes off the road to shoot him a surprised look.

"On Stone." He nodded before starting to roll another wood. "And it's crazy cause I can't even pinpoint who it is, cause Blake and KD both been on some snake shit. Them niggas slimy as hell. KD came to the trap and tried to get me to have one of my guys clap Blake and collect the bread King nem got on him."

"What the fuck be wrong with you young niggas?" Cordale asked, twisting his face up like he just drank something sour. "It's like Loyalty don't even exist no more, it's cool to be a snake. If you not about that backdoor shit, then you a lame. That shit weird as fuck to me, bruh. Back in the day we was killing niggas for showing signs of being disloyal. That shit was frowned upon," he said with a frown like the thought of a snake ass nigga put a bad taste in his mouth.

"I don't understand that shit either, cuz."

"I put them niggas in positions where they gone forever have a bag and all I ever asked for in return was loyalty. My operation was one of the best on this side of the city, until I left them in control, now look at my shit. Niggas scared to hustle on the block because they got so much goofy shit going on. They fucked everything up with all these wars and shit," Cordale said, he was steaming. This was his first time voicing how he felt about the state of his empire. "We gotta figure this shit out, lil cuz, and if we gotta cut them niggas off just to repair the damage they caused, then it is what it is."

"I'm with whatever you on, big cuz, just let me know," Von D replied before flaming up his wood. They rode around serving and plotting on their next move.

***

Aisha stood in the kitchen making dinner for Blake, he was out of the hospital and had been at home with her since then. She was happy about that and was catering to his every need, hoping that she made him want to stay in even longer. Her phone vibrated from her receiving a text message. It was from Domo. She almost didn't open it, but curiosity got the best of her, so she did. Her jaw dropped and her heart started pounding out of her chest when she read the text that said, *you looked good standing next to Blake the other day.*

That was more than enough to make her panic. How did Domo know about Blake? She turned off the stove that was boiling a pot of broccoli and rushed to the living room where Blake was playing his PlayStation5.

"Bae, I just got a text from Domo saying that we looked good standing next to each other the other day," she told him, speaking so fast she was stumbling over her words.

"He was probably just tryna scare you, baby," Blake said, consumed in his game of *NFL Madden*, he was playing and gambling and he hated losing, so he was seconds away from dismissing Aisha.

"How does he know your name?" The question hit him like a brick, that was a great question.

"You sure you ain't mentioned my name before?"

"Never."

"Not even on social media?"

"No," Aisha replied, shaking her head. "I'm always careful what I say because I don't want to front you off."

"So, how the fuck do that nigga know my name?" Blake asked, ignoring her shot at him. "Better yet, how does he know you're with me?"

"I don't know but we need to leave. I have to go," Aisha said, letting her anxiety get the best of her. She was starting to become paranoid. She knew that Domo would kill her if he caught up with her. All of a sudden, she felt as if she was being watched at that very moment.

"Slow down, baby, we good here. Ain't nobody been here but yo father," Blake assured her.

"Let's leave, bae... please. If he saw us together, then who knows what he know about you? What if they followed us?"

"It's cameras all around the house, bae, any movement detected sends a notification to my phone. If a mouse run by too fast, I'ma be alerted. We good, baby, do you think I'd let something happen to you?" Blake asked, pulling her down on his lap. Her eyes were watery, and fear dominated her expression. He didn't like how shook this Domo nigga had her. "*FaceTime* him," he told her.

Aisha looked at Blake like he was crazy. "Why?" she asked.

"Just do it," he replied sharply and she did as she was told. Domo answered the call, smiling into the camera. His smile slowly faded when he saw it was Blake in the camera instead of Aisha.

"Fuck you *FaceTiming* me for, bruh?" he snapped.

"I'm tryna see what's up."

"Aisha know she got something that belongs to me, and I want my shit back."

"That shit dead, gang, I ain't gone lie to you," Blake replied with a chuckle.

Domo was fuming on the inside but outwardly, he held his composure. The only thing that gave away his anger was the slight twitch in his left eye. "That bitch probably got you fooled, bruh, but I know my bitch," he told Blake with a small smirk. "See, she know if she don't got every dollar of my money, and every last one of them pills, I won't stop until I get her. And when I get her, it ain't gone be nice. She know my work firsthand," he said and Aisha cringed. She hated his cockiness, but her fear overrode her hatred at the moment, due to the fact that every word he spoke was the truth. He had done some wild shit in front of her.

"I'm telling you, that shit gone, buddy. We was having a drought on real Percs in the city until she came along and fixed that." Blake laughed "We been running through that shit, Gang," he said. He could tell he was starting to get under Domo's skin.

"I can't wait to cash in on that half a ticket you got on yo head," he said, knocking the smile off Blake's face. "Uh, 79th, 83rd and 106th... we gone stalk every one of them blocks until we catch yo yellow ass bruh," Domo said, letting him know he knew a little bit about him. Blake's demeanor shifted he wasn't as arrogant as he was a minute or two ago.

"You not gone catch me loafin on no block, stupid ass, try again," he replied. Anybody could've done a little homework and found out he was from 79th and had Mob ties with 83rd, but for Domo to mention 106th meant he did more than a little homework. That wasn't a block where he hung out a lot. Not too many people knew about his ties to D Block.

"We most definitely caught you out there laughin and shit but you got saved, but next time..." Domo shook his head slowly. "Yo ass dead, bruh."

"Think it's sweet if you want to and yo ass gone be going back to Memphis in a box," Blake promised before hanging up on him. "Fix yo face, baby," he told a frightened Aisha. "You good, I promise," he said and he meant it.

The next morning, Blake had Wet Em Up pick up a hundred pounds from Blue's people, and dropped the rest off to Blake, who wanted to give his leg a little minute to heal up so he was still in the house. Cordale had asked for the pounds because he wanted to get the block back pumping. He felt like he was above selling pounds off his phone. He hadn't hustled like that in over fifteen years. He was a boss, niggas worked for him, that's what he was accustomed to, and he wasn't going back.

Blake tried to convince him to leave the block alone, due to the fact that the Kings aired that bitch out every chance they got. It was too dangerous to play the hood, but Cordale wasn't trying to hear it. He had an old school way of thinking like people still played by the same rules, he thought the respect that came attached to his name still meant something in the streets. It may have to a few people but to most it didn't.

Cordale decided to pull up on Chito. When he made it to his front door, he was searched and relieved of his gun. Inside the home, Chito and Ice were in the living room waiting for him. Chito showed nothing through his facial expression, but Ice had his face screwed up surely ready to kill Cordale the moment Chito gave the ok.

"Tequila?" Chito asked Cordale, raising his glass in the air.

"Naw, I ain't come to kick it, bruh I came to iron this shit out, so we can get back to the money," Cordale replied, helping himself to a seat on Chito's sectional couch.

"Talk, I'm listening," Chito said, before knocking down his shot of tequila and pouring himself another shot.

"We need to come to some type of understanding so we can get this money train rolling again. My brother took advantage of our relationship and used my name to get a load from you. He knew he could run off with the load and my peoples would have to deal with the consequences of his treachery. Ladale was the sole cause of this situation, and I've handled him personally."

"How?" Ice asked.

"It doesn't matter how I did it, all that matters is that he's no longer with us and I made sure of that."

"Let me ask you something, Cordale, what does that solve?" Chito asked.

"He was the one who wronged you and I took care of him. That should make us even."

"How?" Chito asked with a frown. "He wasn't the one who pulled the trigger and killed my brother, that was one of your guys. It's deeper than the drugs I lost. I got the money back from your peoples, we could've walked away and left it at that, but your peoples had to pull a stunt," Chito said, he was starting to feel the shots of tequila kick in. Part of him was getting emotional thinking about his little brother and another part of him was becoming angry, he was starting to see red.

"I lost my brother, just like you did, so I feel your pain. What I'm trying to figure out is, what could I do to fix this?"

"Give me Blake, Von and KD. My problem isn't with you, it's with them. Until those three are dead, my men are gonna keep coming."

"I can't," Cordale shook his head. "I can't give you them, they're the only family I have left. I can't give you them in any shape, form or fashion. Make this the last time that comes out your mouth to me!" he snapped.

"Who the fuck do you think you're talking to?" Ice gruffed, jumping up drawing his pistol. "You come in here talking like you make the rules," he said, smacking Cordale across the face with his gun.

"Ice," Chito called out calmly, stopping Ice from hitting Cordale again. Ice mugged Cordale but stepped back. He was ready to lay him down right there in Chito's living room. Chito knocked down another shot before speaking. "The only way for this war to end is their lives, it's nothing else that can be worked out," he said firmly.

Cordale was hurting, not physically, but his pride was bruised. No man had ever been gangsta enough to pistol whip him. He stared at Ice with hatred in his eyes. "Say less," he said to Chito without looking at him, he couldn't take his eyes off of Ice. He got up and escorted himself out of the home.

Molotti

Chapter 11

It was a cold December day and Cordale had convinced KD to hop in traffic with him, they rode around talking for an hour before he pulled up to his home in Forest Park. When they entered the house KD was caught off guard and infuriated when he saw Blake, Wet Em Up and Aisha sitting in Cordale's living room. He instantly recognized Wet Em Up from being in the trap with Von D.

"What type of weird shit is you on?" KD asked Cordale, mean mugging him.

"I'm not on no weird shit at all, bruh," Cordale assured him. "I need to speak to you and Blake so we could come to a understanding. It's too much shit going on for y'all to be into it with each other. This not how Lil Ced would've wanted it so we gotta end that shit today,"

"I don't got shit to say to that nigga," KD spat after glancing over at Aisha, his heart fluttered at the sight of her sitting there looking beautiful as she always did. He still had feelings for her, he was still in love with her and it angered him seeing her next to Blake. "Dude a snake, Unc, and if you gone continue to fuck with him that's on you, but me…" KD shook his head. "Naw, it is what it is when I catch his ass outside of here."

"You ain't gotta catch me and I'm right here. What's up?" Blake said, returning KD's mug.

"Fall back, Blake," Cordale said firmly. You could feel the intense animosity in the room, like two archrivals were standing across from each other, instead of two men who were just the best of friends. "So, you really ready to kill this man, or die trying to, over a woman that doesn't belong to either one of y'all?" he asked.

"It's deeper than him backdooring me for Aisha."

"So, what else did he do to you to have you feeling how you feel?"

"All type of backdoor shit."

"Like what?" Cordale asked, feeling like KD was just talking.

"For one, he killed Knuckles," KD said, holding up one finger. Cordale hadn't heard the story behind how Knuckles died but he knew Blake was involved. He looked over at Blake who was shooting him a look that said he was trying to read him.

"Then Lil Hot got killed while they were together, his boy Suemoo dead, and he been fucking with that nigga Blue hard as hell, like he not a real opp," KD had four fingers up. "On folks nem grave, that shit weird as hell, bro. Y'all acting like y'all don't see it."

"First off, I told you niggas that shit with Knuckles was some flukey shit, he jumped in front of the Drac while I was blowin. Secondly, Lil Hot let them niggas hawk him down and as far as Suemoo, I haven't even seen folks since he got out the hospital. For all I know, you smoked him cause you knew he was fuckin with me. All the dirt you tryna put on me might be to cover up how you really comin. I'm startin to think it was you who gave the Kings, my Lo, and got folk nem hit up. It's funny they didn't know where I laid my head until I got into it with you," Blake said. This was his first time voicing what he thought. He didn't know if he was only saying it out of anger that KD was accusing him of so much snake shit, or if he really believed it.

"Fuck outta here," KD said, smacking his lips.

Cordale shook his head in disgust. "See, y'all don't even have a valid reason to be into it with each other. We can sweep this shit under the rug and get the block back in order," he said.

"It ain't just me doe, Unc, it's the whole hood. We all feel the same way about dude, that nigga can't come back through the hood."

"Who can't?" Blake asked, turning red.

"You—"

"Man, on my brother grave, you niggas got me fucked up. That's my shit and I'ma come through whenever the fuck I feel like it," Blake snapped.

"On Lil Ced, you not welcomed in the hood, boy. That's not yo shit, yo ass better start playing 47th or the Hundreds," KD replied, shooting a mug towards Wet Em Up. He knew them niggas from D

Block were fucking with Blake harder than they let on and seeing them together confirmed his suspicions. Wet Em Up had officially made the list.

"On my brother, I see I'ma have to spank one of you hoe ass niggas."

"Or get spanked," KD shot back with a smirk. "We on yo ass, boy."

Cordale listened to them bicker back and forth until he couldn't take it any longer. "Both of y'all shut the fuck up!" he barked. "I don't know who the fuck y'all think y'all is, saying who can or can't come through the hood without getting my say so. That's my shit! What, y'all done forgot?" he asked, looking from Blake to KD. "I put you niggas in position and y'all burned my shit to the ground. Can't neither one of you niggas come through the hood until I say so."

"What?" KD asked, screwing up his face.

"You heard what the fuck I said, nigga. You got a problem with it?" Cordale asked, stepping in KD's face. KD did indeed have a problem with what he was saying. He may have been the man with the money, but KD was the face of the hood. He was the one who instilled fear in their opps. Cordale wasn't the one putting pressure on niggas, he was. He wanted to voice his opinion, but he knew if he were to check Cordale, Blake would take advantage of the situation and get on his ass. He was outgunned so he tucked his pride and bit his tongue. "I thought so," Cordale said. "Now get the fuck outta my crib, all of y'all," he said, dismissing everybody.

When everybody left, Cordale rolled up a wood and called one of his lady friends over. He needed the weed to relax himself and once he was nice and high, he would take his anger out on his friend Diamond's good pussy. Drugs and pussy always relaxed him and lightened his mood. He hated how he had to come at Blake and KD, but he was taught that if your right hand sinned against you, cut it off. Blake and KD were moving wrong, and he couldn't let them further destroy the gold mine he created.

If they didn't have enough love and respect for him to squash their beef on behalf of him, then he had no sympathy for them and no regret behind the decision he made. Sometimes a leader had to make those type of hard decisions and put the hood first, that's what separated the Indians from the chiefs. He felt like being cast away for a while would make them come to their senses and see things his way. He just hoped with all the backdoor shit they were accusing each other of, one of them didn't turn full renegade against the hood. If so, he would be the one who put an end to whoever it was.

***

Ice sat in a stolen car with Mo Money, Bang and Domo. They had gotten a call with Cordale's whereabouts and were now sitting outside of his home. Ice's eyes were bloodshot red due to the amount of coke he had snorted, plus the amount of crying he had been doing nonstop since getting the news that Carlos had gotten gunned down. When Carlos' friends claimed he had been killed by a black guy, Ice knew where it had come from. It was as if God had owed him a favor because now, their inside source had given them Cordale's location. Initially, Chito refused to greenlight a hit on Cordale, but how could he deny Ice the opportunity to avenge his son? He couldn't, so he put a hundred thousand dollars on Cordale's head, just so Mo Money and Bang would assist Ice on his mission even though he would've done it on his own and for free.

"Let's go," Bang told everybody before putting on his shades and hopping out the car.

***

Cordale laid on top of Diamond, hitting her with long strokes, he was sweating and breathing heavily. The pussy was so good that he silently prayed he never busted his nut. A thud made him pause mid-stroke. "Go see what that was," he told Diamond, rolling off of her and grabbing his PSD boxer briefs. Diamond put on a robe and left out of the room to go downstairs.

Moments later, when Cordale heard a gunshot, he grabbed his phone and *FaceTimed* Blake before flicking off his bedroom light. He grabbed the two guns he had in the room, a Glock 19 with a switch that was resting on his nightstand and a Glock 22 with a drum on it that he had under the bed. He quickly ran to his walk-in closet and crouched low with his gun aimed. He could hear whispers and multiple pair of footsteps creeping through his home. He looked at his phone to see that Blake hadn't answered, so he hurriedly sent a text to Von D, saying somebody had run in his home and to come over ASAP, before he locked his phone to make the screen go black.

It seemed like he waited for an eternity before the intruders started to close in on his hiding spot, he waited patiently. He thought by the way his heart was beating so loudly, they would hear exactly where he was, he stilled himself and was almost scared to breathe. He had the sliding door to his closet slightly open and his gun aimed out with his finger wrapped around the trigger. The room was pitch black, so he wasn't worried about being spotted. One thing he knew for certain, the first person who entered his room would catch every shot out of his Glock 19.

When he heard footsteps approaching the door he stiffened up, it was go-time, and his heart was beating a mile a minute. He was never a killer but when you put a dog in a corner, he was forced to bite.

The first thing Cordale saw was a green dot hit the far wall of his room, then heard the sounds of someone trying to tiptoe in, one foot at a time. He waited until he could hear the guy breathing right above him before lifting his gun and squeezing the trigger. The switch made his Glock shoot like a fully automatic. Whoever the guy was in front of him, slammed into the door before crumbling down to the ground. The other men took off scrambling, trying to avoid the armada of bullets.

Cordale dropped his Glock 19 and picked up the Glock 22 before bolting out the room. The rest of the house wasn't as dark as his bedroom, so he wasn't cloaked with the shadows. Some type of assault rifle went off as he bolted towards the stairs at the end of the hallway. He wasn't sure if he was getting shot at with a Draco or an AR-15, either way, he wasn't trying to get hit.

He twisted his body in an attempt to turn and send a few shots, but a bullet slamming into his torso made him trip over his feet and go crashing down the stairs. His head slamming to the floor with force dazed him, but a bullet smacking the floor next to his head immediately shook the cobwebs out of his head. He scrambled on his hands and knees, trying to get to his gun which had flown by the couch.

Before he could make it to his gun, he bumped into somebody's legs. He looked up and saw a diamond-toothed smile underneath the ski mask the man wore. The guy put the barrel of his gun on Cordale's head and pulled the trigger. Cordale's brains jumped out of his skull, and he crumbled to the ground.

"Go check on King," Bang told Mo Money. Mo Money was still weary of Bang, so he wasn't moving how he normally moved. The only reason he was there was because Chito paid for their services as a team.

"That nigga ain't came out that room since he went in there, what that tell you?" Mo Money asked, frowning behind his mask.

"We can't just leave him, and he might still be alive."

"Well, go check on him," Mo Money replied. Chito had gotten him that list he asked for and come to find out, someone had recently dropped two hundred fifty grand on his head, on top of all the other bounties that were on him. Someone could collect a pretty penny by knocking him off and that
had him suspicious of everybody, especially Bang. For as much as he loved Bang, the sad reality was that Bang was just like him, slimy as hell. Cutthroat. A snake, so he had every right to be cautious around him.

Bang smacked his lips and headed upstairs. When he got to Cordale's room, he saw Ice sitting down, leaning against the wall gasping for air. He had multiple bullet holes in his upper body. Bang thought about helping him up, but he knew moving him could be fatal. Before he could formulate a real plan, a hand reached past him and shot Ice in the head twice.

"We gone man!" Mo Money barked before jetting out of the house. He ran to their car and jumped in the backseat. Bang hopped in the driver's seat and as soon as Domo closed the door, he sped off. As they sped away from the crime scene a black SRT Dodge

Charger flew past them, followed by a Dodge Durango. "Get outta here, Law!" Mo Money said, sensing trouble behind the tinted windows of both vehicles that had just blown past them. Bang mashed the pedal and did exactly as told.

***

When Blake and Aisha pulled up to Cordale's house and saw Von D standing in front with his face wet with tears, Blake's heart started thumping and a lump formed in his throat, he knew what it was, just off Von's vibe. When Aisha got out of the car, Von D wrapped his arms around her.

"What's wrong, Von?" she asked, already knowing the answer. Von D didn't respond, he couldn't, the sobbing he was doing wasn't allowing him to answer. She shook him off of her and ran inside the house. She stopped in her tracks when she saw her father in the living room laying in a puddle of blood. His blood. The river of tears that escaped her eyes paraded down her cheeks and dripped from her chin down to the chest of her Gucci tee.

Her father couldn't be dead, not when they had so much catching up to do. Not after he promised her years and years of them strengthening their bond. They had made so many plans for their future together. They needed each other so badly. Cordale filled in for the mother she had lost, and she was his second chance at being a father. Aisha cried and sobbed uncontrollably, unable to take her eyes off of her father's dead body. The pain was so immense that she was having trouble breathing.

As if on cue, Blake came in and wrapped his arms around her, he was crying too. She laid her head on his chest and could feel his heartbeat. "I'm sorry, baby," he told her, kissing the top of her head. To him, losing Cordale was like losing his biological father. Cordale had raised him and taught him everything he knew. Cordale was his family.

Blake let Aisha go and went to the second story of the home. He upped his Glock when he saw a foot hanging out of Cordale's room, he slowly approached the room with his gun pointed and was shocked to see King Ice laying there lifeless. He smiled triumphantly. At least Cordale took one of them pussies with him. Ice was one of the main ones they needed to get out the way, he was the muscle, the one who was really bringing the smoke. Now he wasn't shit but a new pack they would be smoking on later. Blake rushed out of the room, back down the stairs into the kitchen to see Diamond laying in a pool of blood. His heart went out for her, she was a cool chick and really loved Cordale.

"Blake!" Aisha called from the living room, making him almost run to her.

"Yeah, bae?" he asked and she handed him her phone. He looked at it to see a text from Domo that said, *it was nice to finally meet yo pops*, with a whole bunch of laughing emojis. Blake knew for sure the Latin Kings were to blame for Cordale's murder, but how did Domo know about it so quick? The police weren't even there yet. Then he said it was nice to meet him, when did they meet?

"He had something to do with this," Aisha whispered. She was such an emotional wreck that her body was trembling. "This is all my fault, I think we should just give him what he wants," she said sadly.

"And what would that change? Who would that bring back?" Blake asked sharply. Aisha didn't respond, she just fell into his arms and cried while he held her tightly.

When the police and paramedics arrived, the police questioned Blake and Aisha, but they knew nothing, so they weren't any help at all. One detective pointed out that Cordale had security cameras in the house, as well as the front and back of the home. But the security system was no good to the cops, because Blake had removed the memory card moments before the police arrived. Once the cops left, Blake reinserted the memory card. Aisha knew the password to Cordale's laptop, so she was able to login and check the cameras' security feed. One video showed four men entering the home, three of the men had dreadlocks hanging out of their ski masks, so Blake assumed they were black men.

Aisha saw the option to view the feed from more than four different cameras, she clicked on camera number three, and it showed the basement of Cordale's home. Camera number five showed the upstairs hallway, they watched the four men creep through the darkness, and the flash from Cordale's Glock light up the hall when he shot Ice.

"Look," Blake said, watching Cordale run through the hall, only to get shot by one of the men who was cradling a Draco. Aisha clicked on camera number seven, which showed a view of the living room, that's when they watched one of the masked men shoot Cordale in his head. When Blake saw two of the men heading back upstairs, he told Aisha to go back to camera number five. He watched one of the men shoot Ice a couple times and that threw him for a loop. He took the laptop so he could go home and watch the videos in peace.

Later that night, Blake was laid up with Aisha while watching Cordale's camera feed. Neither of them had stopped crying, but he was trying to be strong for her. She was really going through it, and he felt her pain. They both felt all alone. Jala had tried to come over to comfort him, but he made up a weak excuse, saying he was about to go out and slide. He really just wanted to be there for Aisha during the time she needed him the most. He wasn't going to leave her side tonight.

As Blake watched the video of one of the masked men killing Ice, he couldn't help but to wonder why. If they came together, why would he kill him? Who were the dreadheads? He had Aisha watching the videos, studying the body language of each dreadhead and she said one of them did move like Domo. If it was him, how was he connected to the Latin Kings? That was another question he sought the answer to. "I think you was right," Blake told Aisha, closing the laptop.

"About what?" she asked, snuggling in next to him. His embrace was warm, the type of warmth that calmed her soul. She felt secure in his arms. Protected. In a world full of problems, she felt problem-free in his arms.

"Leaving the city."

"But where would we go?"

"Cali, Miami, Atlanta, shit... we got enough bread to go anywhere, start us up a business and fall back," Blake said. This was something he had been giving some deep thought to, he was tired of Chicago, and he didn't see himself living to see the age of thirty if he stayed in the city. It wasn't too many niggas of his caliber that lived long, healthy lives, so he wanted to get away while he could.

"Cali would be perfect. I could take some modeling classes and try to get into modeling or acting while we're down there."

"That'll be a good look for yo sexy ass," Blake said, before leaning in to give her a kiss on the lips. For the first time, he realized just how much he was in love with her. He was ready to run away with her and leave everybody and everything behind.

"When do you want to leave?"

"Let me tie up a few loose ends and we can leave as soon as possible, maybe in a week."

"Ok," she replied, giving him a kiss. "I love you."

"I love you too."

Chapter 12

Von D sat in his Dodge Charger listening to G Herbo. He was waiting on 62nd and Stony Island, a destination Mo Money had chosen. They were meeting because Mo Money called and told him he had some valuable information for him, concerning his cousin Aisha. When Mo Money finally pulled up, Von D flashed his brights and Mo Money bopped to his car with his eyes darting in every direction, looking for any signs of danger. You had to be on point everywhere you went in the city.

"What's the demo, Law?" he asked, sliding into Von's passenger seat. "You straight? You lookin bad, bro," he said, seeing the sullen look on Von's face as they dropped a gang sign.

"My mufuckin big cousin got killed and that shit fuckin with me."

"That's what I wanted to holla at you about,"

"What's the word?"

"One of yo homies, either Blake or KD, called that play on Cordale," Money said, stunning Von, who looked at him in surprise. "On Stone law," Mo Money added, letting him know he was dead serious.

"How you know?" Von D asked him before lighting up a wood. He felt his blood start to boil, and he needed to smoke. He couldn't believe one of the men Cordale loved and trusted the most was behind his demise. It was crazy because Wet Em Up told him Cordale had told both Blake and KD they couldn't come back to the hood. So, they both had a motive to want him dead.

Mo Money looked out of the window thinking of how much of his hand he could reveal to Von. He knew he was playing with fire due to the fact that he was there when Cordale was murdered, and Von was his blood. "The Kings greenlighted that hit, but only after one of them niggas dropped the Lo."

"And you one hundred percent sure that it was one of them?" Von D asked through clenched jaws.

"On Stone," Mo Money clarified, coming across his chest with his fist. "You know that's how I eat. I know who all got money on they head and I cash they ass in. King nem wanted me to check you and all yo homies in, but I fuck with you so you know that shit was dead, and I didn't feel right tryna check yo homies, so I fell back. But one of them niggas ain't right at all, bro," he said, shaking his head.

"I need to know which one, cause right now I'm feeling like I should clap both of them weird ass niggas," Von D gruffed, before hitting his wood a few times.

"I'd be lying if I said I knew exactly which one of them niggas it is, because Chito wouldn't tell me. I been tryna figure it out doe, because I know if whoever it is would oop Cordale, then they would oop you too, and I can't let that happen."

"So, do you know who killed Cordale?" Von D asked Mo Money, passing him the wood.

Mo Money was hoping he could've avoided this question. He couldn't throw Bang under the bus, he was giving him a weird vibe, but he had yet to do some snake shit so he couldn't say his name. But Domo was a different story. He had no ties to him, and he personally didn't like him. "It was the nigga Domo from Memphis," he told Von honestly.

"How the fuck did he know Cordale was Aisha's pops?"

"The nigga been doing his homework," Mo Money replied after exhaling a lungful of exotic smoke.

"He had to have come with the Kings, because King Ice got smoked in the crib, so how is he connected to them?"

"He probably got wind of the contract," Mo Money replied with a shrug. Von D was starting to blow him with all his detective ass questioning. "He got some people somewhere around here. I'm tryna find out where and I'ma put a play in motion for you, Law," he said. He felt bad for playing a part in Cordale's murder, so to make it up to Von D he was going to oop Domo, or at least try.

"Say less," Von D replied.

"Fasho," Mo Money said, opening his car door. "And be careful when you around them niggas, bro," he warned before climbing out the car and going to his own.

***

Blake pulled up to Von D's trap on 106th and Indiana, followed by Blue. They both climbed out of their cars and hurried into the trap. They had heard stories of how D Block was at war with the whole Hundreds, and they weren't trying to catch something that wasn't meant for them. Von D and Wet Em Up were inside the trap, bagging up heroin. Blake wanted to formally introduce Blue and Von D and give Von the outlet to fuck with Blue without him.

"Aye Von, you remember my boy Blue, right?" Blake asked Von D, taking a seat on the couch.

"Hell yeah," Von D said, looking up from the dope.

"This who I been getting the pounds from. I'm paying two hundred thousand dollars for a hundred pounds and charging him fifteen thousand for a thousand Percs and another five grand for a thousand Xans. I'm bout to shoot out for a lil minute and y'all can continue doing business, without me as a middleman," Blake said, pulling out a wood and unraveling it.

"Where you going?" Von D asked.

"I'm taking Aisha on a lil vacation. She need it, she been stressed and depressed," Blake replied, not saying exactly where they were going.

"When?"

"After Cordale funeral," Blake said, before licking the wood. "Aw yeah, and I been watching the videos from the night Unc got killed and one of the niggas that ran in the house killed King Ice."

"I heard it was some out-of-town nigga who was really looking for Aisha."

"Yeah, he texted her braggin."

"I should have the drop on his hoe ass soon."

"Yeah?" Blake asked excitedly.

"Hell yeah," Von D nodded. "How do you think they got Unc location doe?" he asked.

"I don't know, that's something that been keeping me woke. It's something about that shit that just don't sit right with me."

"Me neither," Von D replied.

"You spoke to KD?"

"Naw but I'm bout to pull up on him after I bag this shit up. What you bout to do?"

"I got some business to handle, I'ma send you Blue number. Just hit his phone whenever you ready to re-up," Blake said, before dropping a gang sign with both Von and Wet Em Up before leaving.

***

A few hours later Von D was meeting KD on 83rd and Vernon. He parked his car and jumped in KD's backseat behind Lil Moe. "What's the word?" he greeted both of them, dropping a gang sign.

"Shit, how you feeling, Gang?" KD asked, passing him a wood and a Bic lighter. This was the first time they'd seen each other since Cordale had gotten killed.

"I'm straight, bro. Just tryna figure everything out," Von D replied after flaming up the wood.

"What's to figure out? The Kings did that shit. Cordale took Ice with him. He was the muscle, so now all we gotta do is keep our foot on they neck while they hurting, and them boys gone tap out. On Lil Ced."

"That shit deeper than that. Blake said the video of them running in Cordale crib showed it was Ice and three dreadheads. I heard some nigga that's in town looking for Aisha, had something to do with that shit," Von D said, studying KD, trying to read his body language.

"Cause of that lick she hit?" KD asked, pulling into the White Castle's parking lot on 79th and Stony Island.

"Hell yeah," Von replied and then went silent while KD served some guy fifty grams of heroin. Once the guy walked off and KD pulled off, he continued speaking. "I'm tryna find out how is he connected to the Kings. They say he some country ass nigga with his mouth bussed down," Von said and KD's eyes shot to the rearview mirror.

"On Lil Ced grave, a nigga with diamonds in his mouth chased me down with a Drac not too long ago," he told Von, turning to Lil Moe. "Remember when they tried to get us in Princeton Park?" he asked.

"Hell yeah," Lil Moe nodded.

"On Lil Ced, dude had his mouth bussed down and he had dreads. It was like he was laughing while he was chasing me down."

"Yeah, On Stone that nigga got dreads," Von said, handing KD the wood. "I'm on his ass."

"So, Cordale ain't have shit in the crib?" KD asked.

"What you mean?"

"He ain't leave no drugs or money in that bitch?" KD asked, looking at the road. If he would've been looking at Von through the rearview, then he would've seen the crazy look he was shooting him. *What type of question was that?*

"Not that I know of."

"We need to go in there and see. It don't make no sense for the police or somebody else to find that shit," Lil Moe chimed in.

"I'm sure Aisha gone go through all his shit, anything that was left in there belongs to her."

"Man, she gone give that shit to Blake hoe ass," KD said, smacking his lips.

Von D was pissed off because this sounded like something KD and Lil Moe had been discussing. It seemed as if they were more concerned with who would get Cordale's shit, rather than the fact that he was gone.

"I was thinking, right? Since Unc gone, I'm next in line to step up for the hood. So, I was thinking about switching everything up and turning that bitch to a heroin block. Fuck the weed and the pills, you can fuck with that shit if you want to, but the hood gone sell nothing but dope. I might even put some crack out there," KD said.

Von D was fuming, this nigga had plans on taking over for Cordale already and the man hadn't even been buried yet. He never once mentioned trying to find the nigga from Memphis, so they could get some get back. That was throwing Von off, it really had him feeling some type of way. His hand caressed the Glock he had sitting on his lap. He was getting a bad vibe from KD and Lil Moe, and he was ready to knock their shit off. "What about Blake?" he asked, just to see what KD would say.

"Ain't shit change, we dunkin his hoe ass first chance we get," KD replied with a snort. "We was really sparin his ass cause of Unc, but he gone now," he paused to make another quick serve before speaking again. "You really need to tell yo homies to fall back from his goofy ass."

"On Stone, stop saying that shit, G… cause I'ma start taking that shit as a threat," Von D snapped.

"If that's how you takin it, then that's on you," KD shot back. "It is what it is."

"Drop me off to my whip," Von D told him, he was ready to take it there with his ass. While they drove in silence, he caught Lil Moe mugging him through the rearview. "What's up?" he gruffed, returning his mug.

"Where all this tough shit comin from?" Lil Moe asked, he had his gun in his hand too. Von D immediately started feeling like they were ready to dunk him. He was outgunned, so he bit his tongue at the moment. He was convinced now that KD was the snake who had been working with the Latin Kings. He was too power thirsty and greedy. Von D couldn't wait to get out of the car. He would've hit him in the back of his head while he was driving, but Lil Moe was on point, both of them were now. Since things were getting heated, he decided to just play it cool.

"I'm saying doe, Von D, you mad at me now? We into it?" KD asked, looking at him through the rearview. All Von had to do was make KD feel like he was on some snake-ass, riding with Blake shit, and he was gone give lil Moe the greenlight to do his ass.

"Naw, we well, Gang," Von replied dryly.

"I was just sayin that yo homie Wet Em Up be with Blake a lot and I just don't want him to catch something that's not meant for him."

"You know what you know Gang, I'ma pull up on him and get in his ear," Von D said as they pulled up to where his car was parked.

"Let's go downtown and get something to eat later on," KD said to him as he climbed out the backseat.

"All well, just hit my line," Von said before slamming the door shut. He started walking off, he wanted to turn around and empty his clip into KD's window, but he could wait. KD trusted him so he would be easy to get up with.

"Man, he with that shit!" Lil Moe told KD as they watched Von D walk to his car. "We should get his ass out the way right now," he urged.

KD watched Von D. He'd only agreed to get up with him because he wanted to pick his brain. He even knew that he and his homies were rocking with Blake tough. And he even knew they were getting their weed from Blue. They were fucking with the opps, and he didn't condone that shit at all. "Not right now, bro," he said. "On Lil Ced, them niggas in cahoots and I know when we can hit them, and kill a few birds with one stone," he said before pulling off.

***

Blake pulled up on Jala in his new matte gray Trackhawk, he entered her crib holding a Birkin bag that cost him about twenty-five grand. He hadn't seen her in a while. and he hoped the gift made up for that. She knew he had been taking a lot of L's so, she wasn't too mad at him. Knowing he would be skipping town on her without so much as a goodbye, he stuffed a hundred thousand dollars in the Birkin bag. The moment she swung the door open and fell into his arms, he knew he had made a mistake by coming over. She had a firm grip on his heart and seeing her, smelling her and feeling her would make it hard for him to actually go through with his plan to leave.

"What's up, baby? You must miss me a lot," Blake smiled, stepping into the home after Jala released him from her warm embrace.

"Of course, I miss you," she replied and he handed her the purse. She was caught off guard by its heaviness.

"What's in it?" she asked, checking out the bag.

"Just a few dollars I need you to hold for me," Blake replied nonchalantly. "I see you and Momma Nicki been doing y'all shit with the food truck," he said. He had bought her a food truck so she could pursue her dreams, and he'd seen on social media that she was getting nice reviews and ratings.

"Yeah, we lit," she replied with a smile, showing her dimples. "My brother and his friends stay coming wherever we're at and you know that brings the crowd. We be selling out so fast, we have to close up and restock two or three times. Blake could see the passion in her eyes while she spoke about her business. The happiness when she told him what kind of foods she served, and what kind crowds she attracted. His heart swelled with pride because he could say he played a part in her happiness.

"That's good, baby. I'm proud of you," he said with a smile.

"So, how have you been feeling?" she asked, lighting up a thick joint stuffed with exotic weed.

"I'm hanging in there, baby, it's most definitely a challenge doe. Some days are harder than others. I'm not ready to bury my big homie. I'm still not over losing Lil Ced and Six, so losing him just really knocked the wind and the fight out of me. I think Cordale was ready to die doe."

"Why do you think that?"

"Because he lost his wife, his son, his best friend and his brother, he was tired of taking losses. I just feel like he's more at peace, now that he's with them."

"What about his daughter? I know she gotta be messed up right now," Jala asked.

"She doing real bad," Blake said, shaking his head. "That shit a be hard for anybody. The only family she got left out here is Von D and you know he ain't in the position to be there for her, how she needs him to be. We're in the process of finding a way where she can be straight on her own."

"That shit is so sad," Jala replied, taking a seat on Blake's lap. They kissed and that one kiss led to an hour-long sex session. Once they were done, they laid tangled up on top of her sheets. Just like that, Blake was ready to stay in Chicago. Fuck Domo. Fuck KD. Fuck Chito. Fuck everything, that's how Jala made him feel.

Staying with her was worth whatever came behind it. She was so gentle and pure, so precious and rare. She made him wish that he lived a different type of life, one where he could be free of all the troubles that came with being in the streets. Laying there with Jala, he was exactly where he wanted to be. It took everything in him to separate himself from her warm embrace, knowing this time was most likely their last time.

"I gotta go drop these pounds off to Von, l forgot I had that shit in the car," he lied, before climbing out of the bed and stretching, before starting to get dressed.

"When am I gonna see you again?" Jala asked.

"Soon," was all Blake could say. He couldn't even look her in her eyes when he lied to her.

"I love you, daddy," Jala purred, puckering up for a kiss.

"I love you more," Blake replied after kissing her lips. As he walked out of the house, he wondered if he'd meant what he'd just said to Jala. How could he really love her, and he was running away from her with another woman? He tried to convince himself he was leaving Jala behind for her own good, but who was he to say what was and wasn't good for her? Maybe deep down he knew he wasn't good for her. Maybe he knew she was too good for him. Whatever the reason might be, he hoped and prayed she found everything she desperately deserved in life.

After leaving Jala's house, Blake stopped by Lil Ced's baby mother Alexis house to drop her off some money. He hated to leave her behind too, but she knew she could reach out to him anytime for anything. He would make sure she stayed financially stable until the day he died, that's a vow he made to Lil Ced that he planned on standing on.

Blake's next stop was to the trap on 106th and Indiana. He pulled up and called Wet Em Up and told him to come outside. When he exited the trap and saw Blake's new Trackhawk, he smiled.

"What's the word, Gang?" Wet Em Up asked, climbing into the passenger's seat.

"Shit, just came through to see what you was on."

"Shit, dumping. You know my motto, 'Hustle through the sun, so at night I can have fun,'" Wet Em Up said and they shared a laugh.

"I got something for you too, Gang," Blake told him, before reaching in the backseat and grabbing a blue duffle bag. He handed it to Wet Em Up, who unzipped it to see a couple Ziploc bags full of pills laying on more Ziplocs that were stuffed with exotic weed. It must've been at least thirty pounds in the bag.

"What's this for?" Wet Em Up asked, zipping the bag back up.

"For you."

"For what, doe?" Wet Em Up asked, niggas didn't just pull up passing out thirty pounds without an ulterior motive.

"Cause for one, I fucks with you. On my brother, you thorough," Blake said and paused to light up a wood. He hit it, let out a thick cloud of smoke and continued. "And secondly, the only reason I'm in position to hit you like I just did, is because Cordale put me in position. He took a chance on me and that shit changed my life. I wanna put you in position to change yours," Blake explained, before hitting the wood again.

Wet Em Up didn't know how to respond because thanks surely wasn't enough. "I appreciate it, Gang," he said as Blake handed him the smoldering wood.

"It ain't shit, bro. Run yo bag up and stand on these niggas' necks. When I hear about you, that's all I wanna hear."

"You sayin that like you ain't gone be right here with me."

"You know what I meant, nigga," Blake replied with a chuckle. Unbeknownst to Wet Em Up, he had fifty thousand at the bottom of the bag, he would see it when he removed the pounds. It was a helluva start up kit for sure. "I gave Blue yo number too and I'll text you his shit. Whenever you ready to re-up, just hit him up, and he gone give it to you for the same price he was giving it to me for."

"Aight."

"I got a few more moves to make. I'll see you tomorrow at the funeral," Blake said, popping his locks.

"Yeah, I'll be there. Stay dangerous, Gang," Wet Em Up told him, hopping out the truck.

"You too," Blake replied before pulling off.

After a long day of making moves, Blake decided to end his night at the cemetery. It'd been a while since he came to kick it with Six, Lil Ced and Shana, so here he was. He knew this would be his last time kicking it with them for only Lord knows how long. His mood was somber but tense. He was just hours away from burying Cordale and as soon as the burial was over, he and Aisha were throwing their phones away and hopping on the road.

They chose to relocate to Miami. The weather was warm and the way of living was luxurious. Blake knew it wouldn't be hard for him to find a connect out there and make himself some money. He had even thought about going legit and opening up a bar or strip club, he had the money to do it, but he would cross that bridge once he got there and got settled.

"Aye listen to this song, lil bro," Blake said to Six's headstone before turning on Lil Durk's, "Headtaps." Nodding his head to the song, he said, "I know this would've been yo shit if you was here. I wish you was still here... I know you would've had some type of plan for us. This the loneliest I've ever been in my life. On the guys, Cordale just fucked me up getting took out this shit like that."

Blake shook his head and took a swig from the bottle of 1942 he had, the burn from the liquor felt good to him. "I'm shooting O.T. for a minute," he said and paused as if he was waiting for a response. "I got to, bro, it's the only way I'ma survive, plus I gotta keep Aisha straight. I'm all she got now. We going to Miami to start fresh. I wish I could take y'all with me, we never got the chance to travel and shit," Blake said sadly. He was silent for a while before saying, "I'm just wondering how long you gone stand there without saying shit."

"I was letting you vent," Blue said, before stepping out of the shadows. "I knew on the night before Cordale's funeral, I could catch you at the cemetery. You love this place," he said, taking a seat on the grass next to Blake and pulling out a wood.

"I had to come holla at my peoples," Blake replied before smacking his bottle again. "All my peoples gone. That shit crazy, I don't know if I'm blessed or cursed,"

"Believe it or not, you blessed, my nigga," Blue replied, handing him the wood. "My pops got out yesterday. He told me to let you know he'll be at the funeral tomorrow. He just wanted to give you a heads' up so your peoples won't be surprised."

"It's cool, ain't nobody gone say shit to him. Everybody knows that once upon a time they were like brothers. It won't be no problems," Blake said, before hitting the wood a few times. "I'm bout to shoot out for a minute. My homie nem from D Block gone be in tune with you, they some thorough niggas that you should lock in with while I'm gone," he said.

"How long you gone be gone?" Blue asked.

Blake's silence let Blue know that he planned on being gone for a while, this wasn't a vacation or a weekend getaway.

"I don't know," Blake finally mumbled. "I just need to get away for a minute and get my mind right. I feel like I'm breaking down and this ain't the city where you can be broken."

"I feel you, where you going?"

"Houston," Blake lied quickly. He didn't want anybody knowing where he was going.

"Go down there and get yo shit together bro. Everything that's here now, gone be here whenever you make it back, so you really won't be missing shit," Blue said. They spoke while smoking a few more woods together, before Blue decided to let him have some alone time.

Blake sat at the cemetery reminiscing for another hour while drinking and smoking, his emotions were starting to overwhelm him, and he was ready to get the funeral over with and end this chapter of his life.

***

Von D sat in the passenger's seat of the stolen Ford Mo Money picked him up in. They were both dressed in all-black from head to toe. Mo Money had called him and told him he had finally gotten the drop on Domo. They were parked on 61st and Kenwood, sitting in front of a crib Domo was supposed to be in. Mo Money made sure that Bang wasn't with Domo. He didn't want to harm Bang, but he had to assist Von D in the problem he was having with Domo. Mo Money had been watching him all day. He knew Cordale's funeral was in the morning, and he wanted to oop him to Von D before the funeral.

After almost an hour of waiting, the front door to the house opened and four men walked out.

"Domo the one with the dreads wearing the red Givenchy hoodie," Mo Money pointed to him. Von D nodded as they let the crowd walk off the porch and past their car. Von D popped out with his twenty-six-shot Glock 21, and began to run up on the crowd, firing shots. Domo took off sprinting up Kenwood. Von D was fast but not as fast as he was, add that to the fact that his adrenaline was pumping out of fear or losing his life, and it was safe to say he wasn't trying to die tonight.

Von D heard multiple guns going off while he chased Domo across 63rd Street, trying to hit him. A car coming out of the alley on 63rd and Kenwood almost hit him, slowing him down. Domo was able to hit a cut and lose him. He was pissed that he had just fucked that hit up. He walked down the block, looking through different gangways, hoping to see Domo trying to hide and catch his breath. He wasn't familiar with the area, so he decided to make his way back to the car. He walked up to Dorchester.

When he got to 61st and Dorchester, he saw a guy wearing a red hoodie shoot out of a cut. It was Domo, looking each and every way for signs of danger. He smiled to himself because he was headed his way. He leaned on a gate and pretended to be on his phone as Domo approached him, walking fast as hell. When he got close to Von D, he started to cross the street. He didn't know who he was but he didn't want to walk past him just off the reputation Chicago niggas had for being on bullshit for no reason at all.

Von slid his Glock out and ran up on Domo, who must've still been watching him out of the corner of his eye, because he took off. This time, Von D was on his ass. Domo tripped over a bike that was sitting in front of someone's house, he didn't fall but he stumbled, and that was enough for Von to close the space between them. He reached out with his left hand and grabbed a handful of Domo's long dreads. He pressed the barrel of his Glock to Domo's cheek and pulled the trigger. He held Domo's dreads while shooting him all in his shit. Domo's face was destroyed by the powerful .45 bullets.

Satisfied with his work, Von D jogged to the next block where the car was. Mo Money was already in the driver's seat ready to pull off. As soon as Von hopped in the car and closed his door, a red Dodge Charger was hitting the block. Mo Money stomped off and the Charger pursued him. He cursed under his breath, because he knew the driver of the Charger was Bang.

Bang whipped through traffic, trying his best to get on the side of the Ford. If it wasn't for the heavy traffic, he would've been all over the Ford. The Ford hit Stony Island and accelerated down the big main street. That was a mistake because it was no way the Ford could outrun the Charger in open space, the Charger was too fast. The Ford stopped at a red light on 79th and Stony Island. Bang dropped his window, ready to shoot. he was behind the Ford about to get next to it, but two undercover Ford trucks were sitting there.

He looked through the window of the Ford and saw a brown-skinned guy, with a small sponged fro, looking at him with a mug on his face. It was the same guy who was on the porch with Blake and Aisha on 106th and Indiana. He tried to see who the driver of the car was, but he couldn't because the driver's long dreads were hanging down over his face as if he was trying to hide his identity.

The Ford made a turn towards the dicks and he kept going straight. He had a face to go with the shooting, so he was cool with that for now.

When Bang kept going, Mo Money released a lungful of air. He didn't feel like banging it out with his boy. He was sure Bang couldn't have known Domo had gotten caught and killed because if he did, he wouldn't have just let them slide. Mo Money hadn't pursued any of the men who were with Domo. He could've and easily killed one of the men, but the Stones from that area were his peoples and this wasn't his fight. He was there to clean up Von's mess if he needed to, but luckily, he handled his business properly.

"Love, Gang," Von D told him when he dropped him off to his car.

"I owed you that one, we even now," Mo Money replied, flashing his signature mischievous smile.

"Just let me know when I can return the favor and be back up one."

"I can tell you how right now," Mo Money replied quickly.

"I'm not oopin Nutso, so don't even ask."

Mo Money flashed that evil smile again before asking, "Aight, so what about Binky?"

"You know I can't do that either," Von D replied with a chuckle. "He get out next month and you won't need nobody to oop him for you, cause he gone come lookin for you on his own. You know he was on yo ass."

Mo Money laughed at that because he knew it was true. Binky was one of the Black Stones from D Block, he was Nutso's right-hand man and he had a name as being a shooter that thought he was *John Wick* and he knew how to make some money. He was a real headache for Mo Money and a problem that had to get solved, more sooner than later. "We'll figure it out, lil bro. Stay dangerous."

"You too, Law," Von D told him before dropping a gang sign with him.

Mo Money watched Von D walk to his car. His problem still wasn't solved because Chito still had the bounty on him. Mo Money was trying to come up with a way to finesse Chito into uplifting the bounty, but he didn't know how. Until then, he would keep his eyes on Von just to make sure he stayed straight.

Molotti

Chapter 13

Blake pulled up to Cordale's funeral in his Trackhawk and hopped out, looking dapper in a Louis Vuitton suit that was tailored to fit him perfectly. He wore a pair of Louis shades to hide his red, tear-filled eyes. Aisha wore a black Alexander McQueen dress that clung to her petite frame. She had been crying ever since she woke up. Neither she nor Blake were ready to say their last goodbyes to her father.

The funeral, which was being held at the church on the corner of 107th and Michigan, was packed with people who Cordale knew from all over the city. He was a good man who was loved by many. Von D sat in the first pew next to Wet Em Up, Boothie and P Ball who were there to support him and to be on point for him, just in case KD and his boys showed up. He'd let them know they'd had words last time he was with him.

A lot of the folks from 79th and 83rd were in attendance, a couple spoke to Blake, but most greeted him with silence and mean mugs. He could feel the animosity in their stares, and he returned their energy with mugs of his own. It was obvious they had let KD get in their ears about him and from the looks of it, it worked.

Blake scanned the room looking for KD or Lil Moe, but he saw no signs of either one of them. He didn't even see D Lo or Lil Trav, and he expected them to be there.

When Willis entered the funeral, along with Blue and Millie, all eyes were on them. Some of the older folks stared at him with hatred in their eyes. The war between their side and 47th Place was a long, bloody one that accumulated a large body count.

Willis approached the first pew and took a seat next to Aisha and Blake. He had never met Aisha, but he could tell immediately off first glance she was the daughter Cordale had told him about. He gave her a hug. His face was wet with tears, he was truly crushed by Cordale losing his life and it showed.

When they were in the feds, they promised that now that their beef was squashed, they would both die of old age. Cordale broke that promise before he could even make it out of jail.

The funeral was a sad one. Cordale didn't have too many family members left in the city, so a majority of people who were there were people he'd made a bond with, in the streets. When the pastor asked if any friends or family members wanted to speak Blake, Aisha, Von D, Willis and a few other people spoke. Everyone who spoke had nothing but good things to say about him.

After the funeral Von D met Blake in front of the church, they embraced in a brotherly hug. "That bitch ass nigga KD couldn't even show up, I think he fuckin with the Kings on some backdoor shit," Von whispered in his ear.

"On my brother, that nigga weird as hell," Blake replied. "I been telling Unc we shoulda got rid of his ass."

"Don't trip. On Stone," Von D paused to flame up a wood. "We gone bump heads with his hoe ass." He looked around before saying, "I smoked that Memphis nigga Domo too."

"Yeah?" Blake asked, shocked.

"Hell yeah, caught his hoe ass last night. On Stone," Von bragged with a smile. He felt proud to have killed his cousin's killer before the funeral, that's what you called get back.

The news made Blake feel like he and Aisha could stick around now, but then he thought about the fact that the Kings still had money on him. "That's what's up. I know Unc proud," he said.

"Aye Blake, drop me off to my whip," P Ball asked Blake, who nodded in return. Blake shook up and hugged Von D before approaching his truck followed by P Ball. Aisha was already sitting in the truck playing with her phone.

"Bae," she said, still looking at her phone.

"Yeah?" Blake asked, straightening his mirrors.

"I'm pregnant," Aisha said, and his jaw went slack.

"How you know?" he asked, and she shot him a dumb look. "Well, I mean, when did you find out?"

"Earlier. I had been feeling sick every morning for the past couple of weeks, so I took a test this morning and the results came back positive," Aisha was saying, looking over at Blake. Something she saw caused her eyes to get big.

"Blake!" P Ball shouted from the backseat when gunshots erupted. P Ball and Aisha balled up trying to avoid getting shot but not Blake he simply turned to look at the gunmen. KD and Lil Moe were hanging out of the windows of a Dodge Charger, both shooting Dracos at Blake's Trackhawk. Bullets hit the truck and windows with a thud. Blake grinned. The truck was bulletproof, an idea he had gotten from Molotti and he was happy he did.

Von D and Wet Em Up returned fire at KD's car and they peeled off. Boothie ran to Blake's truck and Blake popped the locks for him. "Drop me off in the hood, Gang," Boothie said, looking out the back windshield. He had participated in the gunfight too and was looking for the police, who he knew would be on the scene soon.

"Y'all was scared as hell," Blake told Aisha and P Ball with a chuckle. "This bitch bulletproof. I'm on my Young Dolph shit."

"I ain't gone lie, I thought it was over with," P Ball said smiling. He was really shaken up, that was a close call, too close for him. "My car on 114th and State," he told Blake.

Blake rode up Michigan to 113th and then hit State Street, P Ball had him pull in front of a big gray house.

"Can I please use the bathroom?" Aisha asked and P Ball nodded his head. They climbed out the car and he led her into the house. After they entered, P Ball's homie Vic came out of the crib and approached the back window of Blake's truck.

"What's the word, Gang?" Boothie asked, rolling down the window.

"Shit, what you on?" Vic asked him.

"Shit, just came from this funeral. I'm bout to go to the hood for a lil minute, then I'ma hit the studio, what you on?" Boothie asked. Instead of responding, Vic upped his Glock 23 and stuck his arm in the window and started blowing.

Blake was stunned at first, thinking he had just killed Boothie, but the sudden stinging in his back made him look back to see that Vic was shooting at him. A bullet smacking his face twisted Blake's head around. He mashed on the gas and felt two more bullets slam into his back. Vic continued dumping the truck down as Blake fled the scene and crashed into a Blue and white CPD Tahoe on the corner of the block. The last thing Blake heard was Boothie's door open and shut, before it all went black.

The End

Lock Down Publications and Ca$h Presents assisted publishing packages.

BASIC PACKAGE $499

Editing

Cover Design

Formatting

UPGRADED PACKAGE $800

Typing

Editing

Cover Design

Formatting

ADVANCE PACKAGE $1,200

Typing

Editing

Cover Design

Formatting

Copyright registration

Proofreading

Upload book to Amazon

LDP SUPREME PACKAGE $1,500

Typing

Editing

Cover Design

Formatting

Copyright registration

Proofreading

Set up Amazon account

Upload book to Amazon

Advertise on LDP Amazon and Facebook page

***Other services available upon request. Additional charges may apply

Lock Down Publications

P.O. Box 944

Stockbridge, GA 30281-9998

Phone # 470 303-9761

Submission Guideline

Submit the first three chapters of your completed manuscript to ldpsubmissions@gmail.com, subject line: Your book's title. The manuscript must be in a .doc file and sent as an attachment. Document should be in Times New Roman, double spaced and in size 12 font. Also, provide your synopsis and full contact information. If sending multiple submissions, they must each be in a separate email.

Have a story but no way to send it electronically? You can still submit to LDP/Ca$h Presents. Send in the first three chapters, written or typed, of your completed manuscript to:

LDP: Submissions Dept
Po Box 944
Stockbridge, Ga 30281

DO NOT send original manuscript. Must be a duplicate.

Provide your synopsis and a cover letter containing your full contact information.

Thanks for considering LDP and Ca$h Presents.

<u>NEW RELEASES</u>

SALUTE MY SAVAGERY by FUMIYA PAYNE

THE COCAINE PRINCESS 10 by KING RIO

CONFESSIONS OF A JACKBOY 3 by NICHOLAS LOCK

SUPER GREMLINS 2 by KING RIO

LOYALTY IS EVERYTHING 3 by MOLOTTI

BLOOD OF A BOSS **VI**

SHADOWS OF THE GAME II

TRAP BASTARD II

By **Askari**

LOYAL TO THE GAME **IV**

By **T.J. & Jelissa**

TRUE SAVAGE **VIII**

MIDNIGHT CARTEL IV

DOPE BOY MAGIC IV

CITY OF KINGZ III

NIGHTMARE ON SILENT AVE II

THE PLUG OF LIL MEXICO III

CLASSIC CITY II

By **Chris Green**

BLAST FOR ME **III**

A SAVAGE DOPEBOY III

CUTTHROAT MAFIA III

DUFFLE BAG CARTEL VII

HEARTLESS GOON VI

By **Ghost**

A HUSTLER'S DECEIT III

KILL ZONE II

BAE BELONGS TO ME III

TIL DEATH II

By **Aryanna**

KING OF THE TRAP III

By **T.J. Edwards**

GORILLAZ IN THE BAY V

3X KRAZY III

STRAIGHT BEAST MODE III
De'Kari
KINGPIN KILLAZ IV
STREET KINGS III
PAID IN BLOOD III
CARTEL KILLAZ IV
DOPE GODS III
Hood Rich
SINS OF A HUSTLA II
ASAD
YAYO V
Bred In The Game 2
S. Allen
THE STREETS WILL TALK II
By Yolanda Moore
SON OF A DOPE FIEND III
HEAVEN GOT A GHETTO III
SKI MASK MONEY III
By Renta
LOYALTY AIN'T PROMISED III
By Keith Williams
I'M NOTHING WITHOUT HIS LOVE II
SINS OF A THUG II
TO THE THUG I LOVED BEFORE II
IN A HUSTLER I TRUST II
By Monet Dragun
QUIET MONEY IV
EXTENDED CLIP III
THUG LIFE IV
By **Trai'Quan**

THE STREETS MADE ME IV

By **Larry D. Wright**

IF YOU CROSS ME ONCE III

ANGEL V

By **Anthony Fields**

THE STREETS WILL NEVER CLOSE IV

By K'ajji

HARD AND RUTHLESS III

KILLA KOUNTY IV

By Khufu

MONEY GAME III

By Smoove Dolla

JACK BOYS VS DOPE BOYS IV

A GANGSTA'S QUR'AN V

COKE GIRLZ II

COKE BOYS II

LIFE OF A SAVAGE V

CHI'RAQ GANGSTAS V

SOSA GANG IV

BRONX SAVAGES II

BODYMORE KINGPINS II

BLOOD OF A GOON II

By Romell Tukes

MURDA WAS THE CASE III

Elijah R. Freeman

AN UNFORESEEN LOVE IV

BABY, I'M WINTERTIME COLD III

By **Meesha**

QUEEN OF THE ZOO III

By **Black Migo**
KING KILLA II
By Vincent "Vitto" Holloway
BETRAYAL OF A THUG III
By Fre$h
THE BIRTH OF A GANGSTER IV
By Delmont Player
TREAL LOVE II
By Le'Monica Jackson
FOR THE LOVE OF BLOOD IV
By Jamel Mitchell
RAN OFF ON DA PLUG II
By Paper Boi Rari
HOOD CONSIGLIERE III
By Keese
PRETTY GIRLS DO NASTY THINGS II
By Nicole Goosby
LOVE IN THE TRENCHES II
By Corey Robinson
FOREVER GANGSTA III
By Adrian Dulan
SUPER GREMLIN III
By King Rio
CRIME BOSS II
Playa Ray
HERE TODAY GONE TOMORROW II
By Fly Rock
REAL G'S MOVE IN SILENCE II
By Von Diesel
GRIMEY WAYS IV

By **Ray Vinci**
BLOOD AND GAMES II
By **King Dream**
THE BLACK DIAMOND CARTEL II
By **SayNoMore**

Available Now

RESTRAINING ORDER **I & II**
By **CA$H & Coffee**
LOVE KNOWS NO BOUNDARIES **I II & III**
By **Coffee**
RAISED AS A GOON I, II, III & IV
BRED BY THE SLUMS I, II, III
BLAST FOR ME I & II
ROTTEN TO THE CORE I II III
A BRONX TALE I, II, III
DUFFLE BAG CARTEL I II III IV V VI
HEARTLESS GOON I II III IV V
A SAVAGE DOPEBOY I II
DRUG LORDS I II III
CUTTHROAT MAFIA I II
KING OF THE TRENCHES
By **Ghost**
LAY IT DOWN **I & II**

Molotti

LAST OF A DYING BREED I II

BLOOD STAINS OF A SHOTTA I & II III

By **Jamaica**

LOYAL TO THE GAME I II III

LIFE OF SIN I, II III

By **TJ & Jelissa**

BLOODY COMMAS I & II

SKI MASK CARTEL I II & III

KING OF NEW YORK I II,III IV V

RISE TO POWER I II III

COKE KINGS I II III IV V

BORN HEARTLESS I II III IV

KING OF THE TRAP I II

By **T.J. Edwards**

IF LOVING HIM IS WRONG…I & II

LOVE ME EVEN WHEN IT HURTS I II III

By **Jelissa**

WHEN THE STREETS CLAP BACK I & II III

THE HEART OF A SAVAGE I II III IV

MONEY MAFIA I II

LOYAL TO THE SOIL I II III

By **Jibril Williams**

A DISTINGUISHED THUG STOLE MY HEART I II & III

LOVE SHOULDN'T HURT I II III IV

RENEGADE BOYS I II III IV

PAID IN KARMA I II III

SAVAGE STORMS I II III

AN UNFORESEEN LOVE I II III

BABY, I'M WINTERTIME COLD I II

By **Meesha**

A GANGSTER'S CODE I &, II III

A GANGSTER'S SYN I II III

THE SAVAGE LIFE I II III

CHAINED TO THE STREETS I II III

BLOOD ON THE MONEY I II III

A GANGSTA'S PAIN I II III

By J-Blunt

PUSH IT TO THE LIMIT

By **Bre' Hayes**

BLOOD OF A BOSS **I, II, III, IV, V**

SHADOWS OF THE GAME

TRAP BASTARD

By **Askari**

THE STREETS BLEED MURDER **I, II & III**

THE HEART OF A GANGSTA I II& III

By **Jerry Jackson**

CUM FOR ME I II III IV V VI VII VIII

An **LDP Erotica Collaboration**

BRIDE OF A HUSTLA **I II & II**

THE FETTI GIRLS **I, II& III**

CORRUPTED BY A GANGSTA I, II III, IV

BLINDED BY HIS LOVE

THE PRICE YOU PAY FOR LOVE I, II ,III

DOPE GIRL MAGIC I II III

By **Destiny Skai**

WHEN A GOOD GIRL GOES BAD

By **Adrienne**

THE COST OF LOYALTY I II III

By Kweli

A GANGSTER'S REVENGE **I II III & IV**

Molotti

THE BOSS MAN'S DAUGHTERS I II III IV V
A SAVAGE LOVE **I & II**
BAE BELONGS TO ME I II
A HUSTLER'S DECEIT I, II, III
WHAT BAD BITCHES DO I, II, III
SOUL OF A MONSTER I II III
KILL ZONE
A DOPE BOY'S QUEEN I II III
TIL DEATH
By **Aryanna**
A KINGPIN'S AMBITON
A KINGPIN'S AMBITION **II**
I MURDER FOR THE DOUGH
By **Ambitious**
TRUE SAVAGE I II III IV V VI VII
DOPE BOY MAGIC I, II, III
MIDNIGHT CARTEL I II III
CITY OF KINGZ I II
NIGHTMARE ON SILENT AVE
THE PLUG OF LIL MEXICO I II
CLASSIC CITY
By **Chris Green**
A DOPEBOY'S PRAYER
By **Eddie "Wolf" Lee**
THE KING CARTEL **I, II & III**
By **Frank Gresham**
THESE NIGGAS AIN'T LOYAL **I, II & III**
By **Nikki Tee**
GANGSTA SHYT **I II &III**
By **CATO**

THE ULTIMATE BETRAYAL

By **Phoenix**

BOSS'N UP **I , II & III**

By **Royal Nicole**

I LOVE YOU TO DEATH

By **Destiny J**

I RIDE FOR MY HITTA

I STILL RIDE FOR MY HITTA

By **Misty Holt**

LOVE & CHASIN' PAPER

By **Qay Crockett**

TO DIE IN VAIN

SINS OF A HUSTLA

By **ASAD**

BROOKLYN HUSTLAZ

By **Boogsy Morina**

BROOKLYN ON LOCK I & II

By **Sonovia**

GANGSTA CITY

By **Teddy Duke**

A DRUG KING AND HIS DIAMOND I & II III

A DOPEMAN'S RICHES

HER MAN, MINE'S TOO I, II

CASH MONEY HO'S

THE WIFEY I USED TO BE I II

PRETTY GIRLS DO NASTY THINGS

By Nicole Goosby

TRAPHOUSE KING **I II & III**

KINGPIN KILLAZ I II III

STREET KINGS I II

Molotti

PAID IN BLOOD **I II**

CARTEL KILLAZ I II III

DOPE GODS I II

By **Hood Rich**

LIPSTICK KILLAH **I, II, III**

CRIME OF PASSION I II & III

FRIEND OR FOE I II III

By **Mimi**

STEADY MOBBN' **I, II, III**

THE STREETS STAINED MY SOUL I II III

By **Marcellus Allen**

WHO SHOT YA **I, II, III**

SON OF A DOPE FIEND I II

HEAVEN GOT A GHETTO I II

SKI MASK MONEY I II

Renta

GORILLAZ IN THE BAY **I II III IV**

TEARS OF A GANGSTA I II

3X KRAZY I II

STRAIGHT BEAST MODE I II

DE'KARI

TRIGGADALE I II III

MURDAROBER WAS THE CASE I II

Elijah R. Freeman

GOD BLESS THE TRAPPERS I, II, III

THESE SCANDALOUS STREETS I, II, III

FEAR MY GANGSTA I, II, III IV, V

THESE STREETS DON'T LOVE NOBODY I, II

BURY ME A G I, II, III, IV, V

A GANGSTA'S EMPIRE I, II, III, IV

THE DOPEMAN'S BODYGAURD I II

THE REALEST KILLAZ I II III

THE LAST OF THE OGS I II III

Tranay Adams

THE STREETS ARE CALLING

Duquie Wilson

MARRIED TO A BOSS I II III

By Destiny Skai & Chris Green

KINGZ OF THE GAME I II III IV V VI VII

CRIME BOSS

Playa Ray

SLAUGHTER GANG I II III

RUTHLESS HEART I II III

By Willie Slaughter

FUK SHYT

By Blakk Diamond

DON'T F#CK WITH MY HEART I II

By Linnea

ADDICTED TO THE DRAMA I II III

IN THE ARM OF HIS BOSS II

By Jamila

YAYO I II III IV

A SHOOTER'S AMBITION I II

BRED IN THE GAME

By S. Allen

TRAP GOD I II III

RICH $AVAGE I II III

MONEY IN THE GRAVE I II III

By Martell Troublesome Bolden

FOREVER GANGSTA I II

Molotti

GLOCKS ON SATIN SHEETS I II
By Adrian Dulan
TOE TAGZ I II III IV
LEVELS TO THIS SHYT I II
IT'S JUST ME AND YOU I II
By Ah'Million
KINGPIN DREAMS I II III
RAN OFF ON DA PLUG
By Paper Boi Rari
CONFESSIONS OF A GANGSTA I II III IV
CONFESSIONS OF A JACKBOY I II III
By Nicholas Lock
I'M NOTHING WITHOUT HIS LOVE
SINS OF A THUG
TO THE THUG I LOVED BEFORE
A GANGSTA SAVED XMAS
IN A HUSTLER I TRUST
By Monet Dragun
CAUGHT UP IN THE LIFE I II III
THE STREETS NEVER LET GO I II III
By Robert Baptiste
NEW TO THE GAME I II III
MONEY, MURDER & MEMORIES I II III
By **Malik D. Rice**
LIFE OF A SAVAGE I II III IV
A GANGSTA'S QUR'AN I II III IV
MURDA SEASON I II III
GANGLAND CARTEL I II III
CHI'RAQ GANGSTAS I II III IV
KILLERS ON ELM STREET I II III

JACK BOYZ N DA BRONX I II III

A DOPEBOY'S DREAM I II III

JACK BOYS VS DOPE BOYS I II III

COKE GIRLZ

COKE BOYS

SOSA GANG I II III

BRONX SAVAGES

BODYMORE KINGPINS

BLOOD OF A GOON

By Romell Tukes

LOYALTY AIN'T PROMISED I II

By Keith Williams

QUIET MONEY I II III

THUG LIFE I II III

EXTENDED CLIP I II

A GANGSTA'S PARADISE

By **Trai'Quan**

THE STREETS MADE ME I II III

By **Larry D. Wright**

THE ULTIMATE SACRIFICE I, II, III, IV, V, VI

KHADIFI

IF YOU CROSS ME ONCE I II

ANGEL I II III IV

IN THE BLINK OF AN EYE

By **Anthony Fields**

THE LIFE OF A HOOD STAR

By Ca$h & Rashia Wilson

THE STREETS WILL NEVER CLOSE I II III

By K'ajji

CREAM I II III

Molotti

THE STREETS WILL TALK

By Yolanda Moore

NIGHTMARES OF A HUSTLA I II III

BLOOD AND GAMES

By King Dream

CONCRETE KILLA I II III

VICIOUS LOYALTY I II III

By Kingpen

HARD AND RUTHLESS I II

MOB TOWN 251

THE BILLIONAIRE BENTLEYS I II III

REAL G'S MOVE IN SILENCE

By Von Diesel

GHOST MOB

Stilloan Robinson

MOB TIES I II III IV V VI

SOUL OF A HUSTLER, HEART OF A KILLER I II III

GORILLAZ IN THE TRENCHES I II III

THE BLACK DIAMOND CARTEL

By SayNoMore

BODYMORE MURDERLAND I II III

THE BIRTH OF A GANGSTER I II III

By Delmont Player

FOR THE LOVE OF A BOSS

By C. D. Blue

MOBBED UP I II III IV

THE BRICK MAN I II III IV V

THE COCAINE PRINCESS I II III IV V VI VII VIII IX X

SUPER GREMLIN I II

By King Rio

198

KILLA KOUNTY I II III IV
By Khufu
MONEY GAME I II
By Smoove Dolla
A GANGSTA'S KARMA I II III
By FLAME
KING OF THE TRENCHES I II III
by **GHOST & TRANAY ADAMS**
QUEEN OF THE ZOO I II
By **Black Migo**
GRIMEY WAYS I II III
By Ray Vinci
XMAS WITH AN ATL SHOOTER
By Ca$h & Destiny Skai
KING KILLA
By Vincent "Vitto" Holloway
BETRAYAL OF A THUG I II
By Fre$h
THE MURDER QUEENS I II III
By Michael Gallon
TREAL LOVE
By Le'Monica Jackson
FOR THE LOVE OF BLOOD I II III
By Jamel Mitchell
HOOD CONSIGLIERE I II
By Keese
PROTÉGÉ OF A LEGEND I II III
LOVE IN THE TRENCHES
By Corey Robinson
BORN IN THE GRAVE I II III

By Self Made Tay
MOAN IN MY MOUTH
SANCTIFIED AND HORNY
By XTASY
TORN BETWEEN A GANGSTER AND A GENTLEMAN
By J-BLUNT & Miss Kim
LOYALTY IS EVERYTHING I II III
Molotti
HERE TODAY GONE TOMORROW
By Fly Rock
PILLOW PRINCESS
By S. Hawkins
NAÏVE TO THE STREETS
WOMEN LIE MEN LIE I II III
GIRLS FALL LIKE DOMINOS
STACK BEFORE YOU SPURLGE
FIFTY SHADES OF SNOW I II III
By A. Roy Milligan

SALUTE MY SAVAGERY I II
By Fumiya Payne

BOOKS BY LDP'S CEO, CA$H

TRUST IN NO MAN

TRUST IN NO MAN 2

TRUST IN NO MAN 3

BONDED BY BLOOD

SHORTY GOT A THUG

THUGS CRY

THUGS CRY 2

THUGS CRY 3

TRUST NO BITCH

TRUST NO BITCH 2

TRUST NO BITCH 3

TIL MY CASKET DROPS

RESTRAINING ORDER

RESTRAINING ORDER 2

IN LOVE WITH A CONVICT

LIFE OF A HOOD STAR

XMAS WITH AN ATL SHOOTER

Molotti